FIRE MOON DANCE

Fire Jaguars

Nicole Dennis

POLYAMOUR

Siren Publishing, Inc.
www.SirenPublishing.com

A SIREN PUBLISHING BOOK
IMPRINT: PolyAmour

FIRE MOON DANCE
Copyright © 2011 by Nicole Dennis

ISBN-10: 1-61926-091-3
ISBN-13: 978-1-61926-091-7

First Printing: October 2011

Cover design by Jinger Heaston
All cover art and logo copyright © 2011 by Siren Publishing, Inc.

Printed in the U.S.A.

PUBLISHER
Siren Publishing, Inc.
www.SirenPublishing.com

DEDICATION

To all who continue to believe in me. This is for you, even if it is a little racy for my family to read.

FIRE MOON DANCE

Fire Jaguars

NICOLE DENNIS
Copyright © 2011

Chapter 1

Liquid fire burned down her throat. She tossed back another shot of pure Tennessee whiskey. Upending the empty shot glass on the scarred table to join six others, Hillary Kearney couldn't stop the automatic, wishful glance to the door before staring down at the silent cell phone. She tapped one side to send it spinning.

"Damn bastard not call, not coming. Chicken cat. So much for him being an alpha's boy, tucking tail against his belly and hiding at first sign of trouble."

He wasn't going to sweep in through those doors the way he usually did after getting off work. He wasn't even man enough to explain what he did, why he acted the way he did. She was left with no explanation, nothing. Nothing except being on the wrong end of a prank in front of the entire clan.

"Ripe bastard. Wish I could neuter him with my claws." Dropping her forehead on one hand, a long moan escaped with a drunken edge. Hillary picked up the phone. She hit a button to stare at the smiling faces of her and the bastard. A wishful hope after the moon dance had made her click the photo and set it as the dashboard picture.

It was a quarter after one. The bar closed at one, and she continued to sit alone like an idiot, waiting, hoping.

"Stupid Hillary! He's not gonna show."

Shoving fingers through pitch-black curls, she let a cry of frustration sing through clenched teeth.

It was time to face reality.

She was the new cat among the Fire Moon Clan. She had no weight, no say, and not even permanent status since she was only a transfer. Therefore, she was nothing to them and nothing to him. Josh had cut her off without a word or explanation.

At least, she hadn't heard from him since she caught him screwing Belinda against the wall at the last kin meeting. The damn bitch couldn't stop stealing someone else's lover. She needed to screw every tom until she found her true mate. Unlike the rest of the females who waited for their turns to meet an available tom during the moon dance, Belinda went around and slept with anyone she chose and got away with it. Unlike Hillary, who didn't have family and support, Belinda's father was a high-ranking member, close-knit with the High Alpha family. Not that finding her true mate would stop that bitch from messing around.

Pressing buttons, a little hiccup escaping, Hillary deleted the picture and all others of the two-timing bastard. She dropped the phone face down. "Bah, bastard."

Growling under her breath, she looked for another shot of whiskey. Moaning when there wasn't a ready numbing glass of liquid, she waved a hand wildly in the air, calling for another round. She grabbed an empty glass and banged it on the table when no one came over. Twisting her head, she growled again, her jaguar swinging forward.

"Don't you get nasty on me, little cat."

She snarled, lips pulling back to reveal perfect white teeth.

A snarl equal in ferocity and noise echoed her, forced her lips to close. She looked around for the male who strolled forward, answering her call.

"I told you, don't get nasty on me, little one. Not in my bar. I don't put up with shit in my bar. Not from a drunk female."

A frustrated hiss left her. "Bastian! Want 'nother!"

"Forget it, Kearney, I'm cutting you off," Sebastian Haywood said.

"Nooooo."

He shook his head. "Don't whine, little one. I'm not changing my mind. You're cut off." He strolled over, stride long but powerful. Boot heels clicked against the wooden floor of the kin bar, a white towel in his strong hands.

"No 'm not." Her words slurred. A smile curled her lips. Lifting her baby blue gaze, darkened by the surrounding thick black lashes that fluttered, she pleaded her case to the handsome tom and bar owner.

Dressed in a tight black T-shirt with the bar's logo, dark denims, and battered boots, Sebastian was every kin female's wet dream. He made star appearances in many of hers. Oh, yes. There were many nights when she dreamed of this fine kin male instead of the bastard. Dark gold hair hung to broad shoulders calling out for a female to hang on during a slow dance, though a lot of weight and responsibility for the clan easily rested on them.

A smile curled his full lips while he shook his head, stacking the empty shot glasses in a tower with strong, capable fingers. He set a hand on the table, leaned over, scrutinized her with that dangerous malachite gaze, and sniffed. "You're smashed, kitty."

"Not smashed. Want 'nother round, handsome." She tugged his towel from his hand and waved it back and forth while she pleaded silently.

He played tug-of-war with the towel for a few minutes before he snatched it from her hold. Before she could topple out of the seat, he placed a gentle hand on her shoulder and kept her upright. "Easy there, sweetheart."

"Shanks." She shivered at the touch of his hands.

"You can't even sit straight."

"So what? Not yer problem." She held up a finger. "One more."

He shook his head, closed a warm hand over hers, and forced her finger back down with the gentle grip. Bringing her fist up, he pressed a kiss against the back of her fingers.

She purred in utter sensual delight at the play and difference between his firm lips and night's growth of rough whiskers brushing against her fingers. How she wanted to feel those warm lips all over her body. She wanted to meet him in the Fire Moon Dance, but he hadn't taken a turn the last few seasons.

"No more whiskey, Hillary."

"I deserve it. Please, Bastian?"

"No, not when you can't even talk straight. Bar is closed."

A pout pushed out her full lower lip while she yanked her fist from his grip. She banged her fist on the table. The shot glasses wobbled. "I want another shot."

"Don't be a whiny brat. It doesn't suit you."

"'M still here. 'M a paying customer and want 'nother." Tears welled up in her eyes. "Not whiny brat."

"Just upset over a bastard who doesn't deserve you. Thanks to a bit of bad luck, you ended up with him during the dance."

"Stupid dance, didn't want him as partner. I want 'nother."

"Partner?" he asked, raising an eyebrow.

Her pout returned. "Whiskey. Don't wanna feel or think tonight, Bastian."

"No, no more whiskey. I'll give you coffee."

Her nose wrinkled. "Bleh!" She barely noticed how he tried not to snicker.

"What? Don't like coffee?"

"Ruin my buzz. Don't wanna feel, 'member?"

"I do, but I'm not changing my mind. You get coffee or nothing," Sebastian said.

"Not helping me." Ticked off at his stubbornness, she dropped a heavy head on her hands, her fingers tangled within black curls.

"I'm keeping a kin female safe. It's my duty as a tom. You drank more than enough to drown your sorrows."

"Not goin' away…"

"Alcohol won't make the pain go away, kitty, not the way you want it to."

"Have to do something. Need to try and forget."

A warm hand drew through messy curls, smoothing them from her face, making her turn to see who touched her.

"Hillary, *querida*, why are you doing this to yourself? Is it because of Josh? He's not worth the massive headache you're going to have in the morning. We don't want you hurting over him. The little weasel isn't worth your pain, *mi dulce*," Raphael Salazar said, his Latin tone filled with comfort. Unlike his partner, his loafers helped him be quiet as he moved behind her while she tried to cajole Sebastian into another drink.

Everything blew over her as another erotic thought raced through her mind. Raphael Salazar touched her! Finally, his hands were on her. My, oh, my! She had made it to a drunken heaven filled with gorgeous hunks at her disposal!

Here was the other kin male filling her dreams. The other one she wanted to meet across the dance circle, but one who never stood as an available male. Well, damn the both of them for leaving her helpless and available to the likes of Josh!

Moaning at his touch, she blinked and lost herself, like a tabby overdosing on catnip. Another purr rumbled from her throat, her cheek and ear nuzzling against his fingers and hand as they moved through her curls to the nape of her neck. His warmth, his scent was intoxicating, and she could roll in it forever.

"I wouldn't be in this situation, but neither of you joined in the dances. I didn't wanna go with him, never liked him."

"*Gato dulce*," Raphael said, his hand caressing her face. He crouched down next to the bench. "We couldn't take the chance. We're partners. Sebastian and I love one another. Neither of us wanted one of the females."

Her eyelids closed at those words, and her heart clenched. How she wanted them, yet could never touch them, especially outside the season and the dance. "You never danced."

Raphael dropped his gaze. "I couldn't stand the chance of ending up with the bitch."

"Bitch?"

"Belinda," Raphael said. "The other females within her group are equally horrid. No male should have to put up with them as a possible mate."

"Rafe," Sebastian said, moving around until she could gaze at both of them.

The dark-haired tom lifted his head and stared at his partner. His eyes were no longer slumberous, but hard like pieces of coal. "She came on to me, Bastian, at every meeting. The little *puta* made no qualms about it. You think I would dare take the chance of staying a month with her?"

Hillary froze at the scant scent of fear coming off the powerful tom crouching still next to her as he spoke about the female they all hated. Yearning urges rose inside her jaguar. She raised her hand and cupped it around Raphael's cheek, warming the chill, trying to comfort him. She glanced at Sebastian. She saw how his eyes hardened.

Nails turned into claws and dug furrows into the top of the bench. A low, horrific growl rumbled from his chest. "That damn bitch." Sebastian rose, but stopped when Raphael raised a hand and gave a quick shake of his head.

"No, *amante*, we are safe. We found the one we seek."

Sebastian bobbed his head. "Yes, we are safe."

"What? Safe? Who do you seek?" Hillary watched their gentle interaction. It startled her how quickly Sebastian pulled back his jaguar.

"We didn't want the chance of being matched with her, so we held back, waited," Sebastian said.

"Until the right time," Raphael finished.

"Why change your mind now?" Hillary lifted her head.

"We found the one we've been looking for to complete our lives."

The males turned to meet her gaze. Raphael rose to his full height, eyes returning to their hypnotic nature, his limbs graceful while his fingers threaded through her curls. Sebastian moved around the booth as if to block her in on the bench.

Chapter 2

Here she was, in this impossible, drunken situation with the two males she desired most out of the entire kin, and she couldn't do a darn thing about it. She was forbidden by laws to touch or love them outside a match sanctioned by the dance. As a newcomer, she must obey the rules her first three years to gain full status. She couldn't risk everything she worked for on a drunken night of lust. Her father, she needed to remember her father's orders. She couldn't take the chance to disobey him, not ever again.

Blinking to bring the closest face in focus, she noticed it was the olive-toned face, dark hair, and eyes of Raphael and a lusty sigh escaped her. She wanted them, but she wanted to become part of the powerful kin. Her head dropped back to the table with a noticeable *thunk.*

"Ouch," she muttered and rubbed her forehead.

Raphael, the other owner of the bar and Sebastian's partner, slid next to her in the booth. He bumped her hip with a playful grin. "Scoot."

"Nope, I'm quite comfy." She took in the long legs covered in dark denim, but he wore those sensible Italian loafers that let him sneak up on her. The bar's black T-shirt stretched across his muscular shoulders and chest.

"Stubborn little kitty," Raphael teased, bringing Sebastian into the conversation.

"Drunk little kitty," Sebastian corrected.

She reviewed him for the chance. "Want 'nother."

"No."

"You're being so evil to me, Bastian."

"No. It's called being protective of you, little kitty. There is a large difference between the two."

Rolling her eyes, she dropped her head and let out a soft hiccup. "'Scuse me."

The men chuckled at her playful drunken behavior, but she felt safe and comfortable with them. Even as the lust settled deep in her belly, built over the past year of her arrival to the kin and seeing them across the clan house, she wanted this gorgeous pair of males. Yet, due to the archaic partner rules, she couldn't move toward them.

She felt Raphael physically shift her over on the leather seat. Reaching six-two in height and over two hundred pounds, he topped her height by a foot and weight by over a hundred pounds. She couldn't put up a fight against him, even without the alcohol stirring her mind. Her eager jaguar purred in contentment in response to the attentive males. She didn't want male attention. She wanted mind-numbing alcohol.

"Why are you drinking hard liquor? You never drank in such a fashion before when you came here."

Looking up, she tumbled headfirst into Raphael's dark gaze, surrounded by thick charcoal lashes. She had a sudden urge to devour a slice of devil's food chocolate cake. In the depths of his gaze, she saw such opposites: comfort and danger, caring and sensuality, sensitivity and passion. Sometime during the night, he had pulled back the long café noir hair into a ponytail, but she wanted to see it fall free, framing his chiseled face.

"I'll have a piece of chocolate cake, please," she said with a smile, touching a finger to his hair.

"Pardon?"

She shook her head. "What? Oh…" She blushed hard at what she had just said to him. "Nothing. Never mind about the chocolate, stray thought."

"Well? Why did you do this to yourself?" He raised a hand and drew his thumb down her cheekbone. "Normally, you stick with a simple beer and dance with the others, just to have a little fun. You never touch anything like hard 100 proof whisky, *querida*."

"You noticed me out of all the kin who come here? You noticed what I drink?"

Raphael smiled, the smile warming the chocolate of his eyes, adding a sparkle to them. He looked up to his partner and lover, who settled on the bench opposite them.

She turned her head in time to watch an answering smile curl Sebastian's full lips. A golden light warmed his malachite gaze. He raised a hand to slip a few strands of blond hair behind one ear.

"We notice everything going on in our bar."

"I'm one female, still new to the clan and low ranking. No one spec—" She stopped when Raphael placed warm fingers against her lips. She blinked once, twice at the simple gesture.

"Every kin female is unique and special in her way. Never ever doubt yourself or your talents," Sebastian said.

She slid her gaze from him and back to Raphael, wondering how they did this back and forth talking so easily.

"Now, why drink yourself into such a stupor?"

"Wanna forget what happened to me." A slow shrug hitched her shoulder. Her voice fell low and quiet.

"You want to stop yourself from thinking about him? Was he supposed to meet you here tonight to explain himself?" Raphael inquired, stretching out her simple words.

"We were supposed to be together until next moon, but at the meeting—" She shivered hard as she sat up straight against the booth and wrapped arms around her petite, pear-shaped body filled with barely there breasts and full hips. She knew she wasn't much to look at, let alone sexually desired by kin males. Her skimpy, silky tank top didn't show off her assets, but was pretty and went well with her favorite boyfriend-style shorts. Of course, it didn't come close to anything the well-endowed, skinny-assed Belinda could pull off.

"Things didn't work out the way you thought," Sebastian said.

"Nothing happened the way anyone thought." Raphael growled in a disappointed tone. He leaned back against the seat and stretched an arm around her, resting a warm hand on her shoulder to encourage her to lean against him.

Turning her head, she looked at him and then Sebastian, who nodded. Tucking her feet up to one side, kicking off the heels, she snuggled against Raphael's strong chest, breathing in his delicious scent and warmth. Another hiccup and blubber of tears escaped, before she burrowed against his chest.

"He fucked Belinda in front of everyone…" she muttered against his shirt, one slender hand clutching the warm cotton.

"It was a claiming, Hillary. A mate claiming created by the Goddess herself," Sebastian said.

Another drunken hiccup-burp left her. Her ivory skin flushed delicately as the men chuckled. "'Scuse me." She pressed her fingers against her mouth.

"Six shots would do that to any kin lady, even some of the toms." Raphael drew his fingers down her soft hair before burrowing under the curls to find her neck.

A low purring rumbled in her throat when he began to massage the knots. She felt him lean closer and heard him take in a deep breath. She wondered if he smelled the alcohol haze or her natural scent. She prayed it was the latter.

"Six would put out a human male. The whiskey was a 100 proof since nothing else works on our metabolisms," Sebastian said in an impressed tone.

"Why would he do that? At the meeting? In front of everyone? To make a fool out of me?" she cried out, pain filling her voice.

"It's a part of who Belinda is and the weakling nature of Josh. She pushed him around to get what she wanted, to get her position in the kin," Sebastian said.

"But the dances?"

"She didn't care about the progression of the dances. She was her father's child and spoiled rotten since her birth. Her mother died in childbirth, and her father spoiled her. It's the same reason she didn't go to another clan to help spread our genetics, like you accepted the offer and joined ours. Her father didn't want to let her go. Belinda got away with what she wanted, and she wanted Joshua."

"He's the High Alpha's youngest son, even though the Fire Moon Dance matched us during the last season."

Sebastian reached out and caressed her cheek with the back of his fingers. She tilted her head against the gentle touch, a soft purring in her throat.

"You're still a transfer, a new member. There is no way Belinda will let you outrank her by being Josh's mate." Raphael trailed his fingers up and down her spine, warming her skin and body with his touch.

"Were they matched before I came along?"

Sebastian nodded. "The season before you entered, and she played him along since they were children, as she did with most of the toms."

"Though you resisted her games." She scrutinized Raphael and then Sebastian.

"Even though she continued to hit on Raphael, who should have told me earlier about that, we turned to other advances. There weren't as many as you suspect, Hillary. Most females knew we were together and none wanted the stigma of being mated to that kind of tom," Sebastian said, clearing his throat, crossing arms over his chest.

Raphael snorted at the last bit.

"That kind of tom?"

"A tom that sexually and emotionally prefers another male instead of a female," Raphael explained.

Hillary grew quiet at the thought of dreams of being with either one of these delicious men shattering into a thousand pieces. Neither one would ever desire her. No wonder she felt safe. They saw her as a friend, comforted her as a little sister.

"How long did he know Belinda was his mate?" She changed the subject in a harsh way. She straightened from Raphael's side, holding herself away.

She saw the men glance at each other and then met Sebastian's gaze. His eyes reminded her of those popular crystalline aggregates found among copper deposits, polished and carved into jewelry. His eyes were a distinctive bright green and finer than any jewel she had marveled at in the stores. Tumbling headfirst into those gorgeous depths, she loved how long dark blond lashes surrounded them and matched the fall of hair covering his shoulders. His skin was golden, not olive like his partner's, but warm. Over six feet in height, they were wonderfully formed males. Not only were they owners of the kin bar, but powerful warriors for the kin clan. They turned into strong jaguars to run with the rest of the cats. Sebastian became a golden jaguar while Raphael became a black jaguar like herself.

"Tell me, Sebastian," she insisted.

His steady gaze remained impassive, but she could tell he didn't approve of Josh and Belinda's actions. "A while."

"What is a while?"

"A while, Hillary," Raphael answered.

"Then it was during their dance mating, the obvious time for things to become hot and heavy between them for all to notice. That is what the Goddess wills, right?"

"Yes, it would happen that way with a regular couple, but Belinda insisted on holding it off. They fought off the Goddess's blessing until it became too much to bear, which resulted in the frantic mating," Sebastian said.

Hillary turned to Raphael. "Is that true?"

Raphael sighed and confirmed her answer.

"Did everyone know but me?"

"It's only because you were new. No one knew how little your clan tutored you in the way of the Fire Moon Dance and of true mates before sending you to us. How could anyone tell that you didn't know when someone had met their mate?" Sebastian asked.

"Yet if one had met their mate, why would he still dance?" she demanded. "I was told only those still available were supposed to perform. That's what the occasion is for, the potential to meet one's true mate."

"It is, but as the High Alpha's son, Josh must participate. Until he's mated and confirmed, he must dance in all sequential seasons then go off with those matches, even if they're not his mate."

"It was a game to them." She slammed a hand on the table. Her nails lengthened and curled into her claws.

Sebastian reached out and covered her slender hand with his larger one. Leaning forward, he cupped her hand with his and brought it up to place a calming kiss on her palm. He rubbed his whiskered cheek against her sensitive fingers, letting her nail-claws brush, rake his skin. Purring, he continued to rub against her hand, calming her with scent and sound.

She stared at the contrast of the beginning claws grazing the blond whiskers. The roughness of his bristles, the sharpness of her talons, the warmth of his skin, and the sensuality of his gaze all fed into her anger, into her jaguar. She watched her claws retreat back into normal fingernails, and he kissed them individually before suckling her forefinger. Her body shivered at the lavish attention he gave her. Her cat awakened, sexually, lazily, stretched inside her mind, and circled in awareness of these males.

"I was a game. A toy tugged and played by them for their pleasure and whimsy, for their amusement." She straightened from Raphael's side, energy burning away the alcohol as anger built. She yanked her hand from Sebastian's attentions, her fingers tingling from his touch and kisses. She moved to rise.

Raphael's hand gripped her shoulder, enough to keep her against him, but not to cause her harm. Dropping his head, Raphael nuzzled her neck with his nose. He pressed his lips against her neck, purring softly in comfort.

"Shush, calm, *querida*," he whispered.

"Sweet Goddess! No, I can't be shushed! Not after what they did. How could the elders let them get away with this? I'm new to your clan. How many other new females were hurt in such a horrible fashion? How many other new females have you lost?"

Before Raphael could lose his hold, Sebastian moved to her other side on the bench. They sandwiched her in the middle, not letting her race away to tear into the couple with claws and fangs.

"How dare they use me? How could I let them use me? I'm such an idiot, such a fool to believe him, his words, his scent!" she screamed in outrage, pain. Inside her mind, her she-cat howled.

"She has a point, Raphael. Don't calm her. She has a right to be outraged," Sebastian said, rubbing his bristled cheek over her head as she burrowed her face against his neck.

Another cry of pain left her and she bit down on the muscle and sinew of his shoulder. She heard his answering growl of pleasure and knew he enjoyed the playful bite, just as a jaguar would. His hand came up, fingers sliding into her curls, holding her in place.

"There is no room here on this bench. We shall move to the floor, not clean, but safer," Raphael said.

Sebastian growled back in agreement.

Barely aware of their words, Hillary gripped Sebastian's arm with her fingers, nails digging into his thick skin.

The toms wrapped their arms around her, lifted, and carried her to the middle of the dance floor. They settled back down with her between them.

"Go on, kitty, let it out. Let the Goddess hear your anger and need."

With caresses, whispers, warmth, and presence, they let Hillary scream her rage and pain. Pale skin revealed from the skimpy top and boyfriend-style shorts rippled and darkened. Rosette patterns appeared upon her skin as her jaguar came forward, wanting to protect her from this heartache.

"No, *gato dulce*, not that way. Give your energy to us. Let us take it," Raphael urged in her ear, his hands encouraging her to open her eyes.

Feeling Sebastian pull away from her grip, she watched him pull off the black T-shirt with the bar's logo, revealing a rippled belly and muscled torso. She snarled, growling at the masculine sight in front of her. Fingernails again turned into claws to dig deeper into the wooden floor underneath her. Only the warmth and power of the alpha toms surrounding her stopped her turning.

"Touch him, *querida*, touch his chest. Caress him with your energy, your power. You are strong, Hillary. Let him feel you," Raphael whispered, nipped her ear with his teeth, before laving the hurt with his tongue.

Anger turned to passion as her head tipped to the side, black curls falling from her face and long neck, giving Raphael access to her pale skin. Snarls turned to sweet moans when he placed light kisses on the sensitive area. Then he graduated to open lips with tongue and teeth until he circled her ear.

"What are you doing to me?" she whispered, panting against the need.

"Enjoying a beautiful woman in our arms," Sebastian said, kneeling next to them on the floor. Lifting her hand, he placed a kiss on her palm and placed it on his belly.

"What…What?"

Raphael raised his attention from her neck and shifted to where she could look at them. "It's simple. We wish to love you together. Help you forget him, what he did to you."

"But, you're together."

Raphael looked at his partner. Through the fear, the alcoholic fog, and lust, she saw the love and trust flow between the men. "We've been looking for someone to share. A third."

"Our mate," Sebastian added.

"It's simple. We choose you. We searched and found you. We're safe in your arms, like you are safe in ours."

Hillary wiggled out of their grasp and scrambled out of their reach.

"Hillary, *querida*, wait…" Raphael said, holding out his hand.

She held up hers, shaking them.

"Kitty, *por favor*…"

She shook her head.

"Hillary, we're not going to hurt you. We're nothing like that piece of scum." Sebastian rose to a crouch to enclose her, embrace her between them.

Holding a hand to her spinning head, she shut her eyes tight. "Sweet Goddess, this is crazy. Insane."

"What is crazy about our offer?"

"You said you two don't dance because you're partners. Toms who prefer toms," she said. "You don't dance. I can't touch you."

"We don't dance because of Belinda's shenanigans, because we fear being attached to her for a month. We never danced because we never saw a female we wanted to share our life with until we saw you, but then we needed to wait, to find a way to connect you to us without her interfering."

Raphael shivered. Sebastian laid a hand on his partner's shoulder.

"Since your arrival in kin, we have felt your energy, breathed in your scent, and adored your light. We watched your dance and wanted to be a part of every dance."

"Why didn't you?"

"Her, it's because of her and the others like her." Raphael ran a hand through his hair in a frustrated motion. "There's no way we wanted to take a chance of being with one of those *putas*." He spat on the floor in disgust.

"Raphael, please," Sebastian said, warning his partner, who let out a low growl.

"She needs to know the truth." Another fierce growl escaped, echoing through the empty bar.

Hillary jumped at the growl, glancing nervously between them.

"I must admit though, he is right, Hillary. There are rumors she fixes the dances to get the matches she and her friends want. If we joined in, there would never be the chance we need to make things right." Sebastian lifted his fingers to trace her cheek, felt her trembling.

"We wanted to rip apart every tom who dared to dance across to you and match you, which is why we needed to find a way to get around her and beat her games."

"Raphael, calm down. We found the way, the right way, and there is no need for the anger. She is safe with us," Sebastian finished.

"They never touched me after the dance," she whimpered. "They kissed me once, said I wasn't theirs, and walked away. I kept feeling something was wrong with me."

"No, *gatita dulce*..." Rising, Raphael moved, touching her shoulder, but she shied. "Let us take you home. We'll take care of you. *Por favor*, let us care for you. We need to do this for you, for us. Let us show you how things can be between all of us."

"The rules, the dance..."

"We'll dance this week and be together."

"No, I can't disappoint my father. He sent me here to represent our clan. I can't bring shame to my family by breaking a forbidden rule because I drank too much. I know better." She raced away from temptation.

Chapter 3

Dropping to his knees, Raphael's hands fisted and pounded against his thighs. He screamed in frustration, a flourish of Spanish falling from his lips, hands opening and shoving through his dark hair, skin tightening around his face. He barely noticed when Sebastian crouched behind him, wrapped long, warm arms around him, rocked them, and his evening bristle cheek rubbed against his head. His skin darkened with black rosettes as his jaguar pushed forward. It wanted the freedom of a shift and run through the forest to forget the pain of their mate.

"Dear Goddess, she ran from us! We frightened her, and she raced away." Raphael raised a troubled gaze to his partner over his shoulder.

Sebastian's embrace tightened. Raphael turned, wrapped his arms around his partner. "She doesn't know us. We are two powerful, unknown males, and she's an untouched female. We did come on a little strong, and, it seems, she only knows the rules. She's young, very young compared to our years. Her father must have a great hold upon her life."

"We scared the living daylights out of her. She'll never come near us again."

"Oh, I'm sure she will. Underneath the fear, you can still smell the desire."

"It was divine, so sweet, sultry, and feminine. I never scented anything like her before. Even without the dance, without the mating, I know she is meant for us." Raphael shook his head, his fingers gripping Sebastian's biceps, digging into the skin.

"I smelled the same. Hillary truly belongs to us."

"It makes me want to scoop her up and bring her home. Tuck her in bed between us so we can keep her there forever."

Sebastian laughed and nodded. "I wanted to do the same thing."

"Then how in the name of hell could we try to take our beloved on a sticky bar floor like we truly are the animals humans call us? How could we do that to her? Our beloved?"

"Rafe, please, don't beat yourself up. It was a wicked combination of us pure, punch-drunk high on desire and need from her scent and the urge to mate. We didn't handle this night right. It was all unexpected and Hillary's drunk," Sebastian said, rose, drew Raphael to his feet.

"It doesn't excuse our horrible manners and manhandling. She's our mate, our *pareja*."

Sebastian nodded.

They went through the motions of cleaning the last of the tables and moved to the bar. Raphael slammed a hand on the bar and then dragged fingers through his hair. He dropped heavily onto a bar stool while his partner went through the closing procedures at the register.

"Calm down. Don't get yourself so agitated."

"We can't lose her, Bastian. I don't want to lose her," he said, fear coursing through his body, shaking heavily on the stool.

Listening to his partner, Sebastian set his work aside. He placed a glass of cranberry juice in front of him. He caressed Raphael's forearm with a light touch of his fingertips. "Here, take a few slow sips. You need to calm your jaguar. I can feel him brimming under the surface, ready to explode out of your skin."

"Who cares if he's pacing? I want to break out and race after her! Either that or a night at Twilight."

"I'm sure Xavier would love to see us, but not if you're on edge. You know the rules of his club. No claws or fangs," his partner said, reminding him about the upscale fetish club just outside the clan limits.

"The energy there would pull back the jaguar." Raphael spun the glass between his fingertips and grinned at the thought of their elegant friend. "You know Xavier would adore her if we ever brought her there."

"Hell, he would take her away from any cat the minute she stepped into his club. Screw the laws of the clan. Hillary is just his type—curvy, innocent, feisty, and pure natural beauty." Sebastian shook his head as he flipped through the last of the receipts.

"Then we better not bring her there until we're sure she is ours. We need to go after her! How could we let her go like that? It was foolish of us."

"We're not going to lose Hillary. Not to Belinda, not to the rules, not to any of the other males."

"How can you be so calm and assured? You're always so laid-back, a flipping iceberg at times. Just when we found her, she slipped from our fingers. We've been out of the game for a while, you and me. Xavier will question whether we know what to do with her. *I* wonder if we'll know what to do with her." He sipped the tart drink, swirling it in the glass, staring into the deep red liquid.

"I know we're not going to lose our Hillary. Relax, my passionate Latino jaguar, everyone knows not to tangle with us. Of course we will know how to love her."

Raphael made a rude sound and glared at his partner. "How can you possibly know such things?"

Sebastian leaned back against the bar, crossed his arms over his chest, and shrugged. "A plan is forming in my mind."

"A plan?"

"We confirmed there is something between us tonight. Yes?"

"Barely, Bastian. We never kissed her, tasted her, or touched her. I ache to hold her close, embrace her tight, and devour her. I desire to know her very essence."

"Now that might scare her off again." Sebastian chuckled and ducked when Raphael grabbed the towel from the bar top and tossed it in his direction. He held his hands in an innocent position.

"When were you ever innocent?"

"Hmm? Before I met my powerful, passionate Latino jaguar who pulled me to the dark side. Weren't you the one to introduce me to the pleasures of Xavier and his club?"

"You enjoyed every minute of the introduction and keep enticing me back to Twilight, so don't go blaming me for that dark path we both love," Raphael said, wagging a finger.

"I'm not even sure when I was a cub I could be called an innocent." Walking down the bar, Sebastian leaned over and planted a hungry kiss on Raphael's full lips.

Threading fingers through Sebastian's hair, he held him in place, opened his lips, and slicked his tongue against his lover's palate. When the other man moaned in need, Raphael nipped at the lower lip and laved it with attention. Pulling back, he stared into those familiar green eyes.

"We never kissed her, our *querida*," Raphael said, fingers tracing swollen lips.

"We will."

"How? How do you know this?"

"I found the way," Sebastian said in that satisfied tone.

When Sebastian wouldn't answer right away, Raphael growled and rose. He stalked and dogged his partner throughout the entire closing procedures.

Even when he followed his partner into their home, he pushed past the stalwart cat. He yanked off the sweaty T-shirt and tossed it on the sofa. Kicking off the loafers, he let them lie where they dropped.

"Where are you going?" Sebastian called after him.

"Outside. Want a fucking shift to get this edge off me since we're not going to Twilight. Are we?"

"Not when you're behaving like this. Xavier will kick your furry butt back on the street until you calm down, or whip you."

"You're not helping matters," Raphael growled back.

"Raphael, wait…"

Stopping, Rafe turned on the balls of his feet and raised a dark eyebrow to take in his partner's lithe figure standing at the front door. He crossed arms over his chest, deliberately letting his muscles pump and flex.

"Fine, you hot-blooded Latino, don't bring any dead things back in the house. I'm not cleaning up the mess this time." Sebastian waved a hand.

Growling, Raphael shoved a hand through his tumbled hair, spun on his foot, and moved. He needed the damn shift and he needed it now.

Yanking at the button and zipper, he shoved the pants over his ass and let them drop with a quiet hiss of fabric. A jaguar's scream filled his mind and came out as his body contorted. Black fur covered his golden skin along with the hidden rosettes.

Bones snapped and shifted as joints and muscles rearranged themselves inside the changing frame from human to jungle cat. Soon, the compact, well-muscled animal stood in the doorway, nearly six feet in length with another two feet added by the swishing tail. Shifting his head, Raphael's golden, dark eyes stared at his partner and lover. He leaned back on his hindquarters as he stretched his front legs, powerful claws appearing from the paws, and then reversed the position to lengthen one back leg and then the other. His tail moved to keep him perfectly balanced.

He shook himself from head to tail and sat on his rump to lick a paw and clean his face, as neat as a housecat. His thick tail flicked back and forth. He stopped when Sebastian crouched next to him, wrapped arms around his stocky neck, and hugged him tight. Turning, he draped his head over Sebastian's shoulder and gave a rough purr.

"Go and have a run. I'll be here later to talk and explain my plan. We're not going to lose her, trust me," Sebastian said when he rose and opened the door.

Rubbing the length of his body against Sebastian's legs, Raphael raced out the door and into the darkness, his dark coat blending into the night.

Chapter 4

Exhausted after the shift, stretching, comfortable in his nudity, Raphael wandered his way through their home to the bedroom. Along the way, he noticed Sebastian had picked up his clothes. It was one of the little things Sebastian always did after a long night at the bar. He was the neatnik side of the partnership while Raphael preferred a couple of piles around him to give things a lived-in appearance.

Scratching his chest, he made his way to the shower. A twist of his hands had the shower running closer to what a polar bear preferred temperature than a jungle-born jaguar. Stepping into the shower, he placed hands against the cold tiles and let the freezing water rain against his heated skin. It continued to calm his jaguar down after the hard shift. Closing his eyes, he let out a frustrated sigh.

There were some things the shift couldn't push off his shoulders and mind.

A low curse forced his eyes back open with a warning growl to the intruder.

"Damn, Rafe, don't start that up. What is it with you and freezing water? Freezing my nuts off and that doesn't do you any good," Sebastian cursed then teased as he stepped into the shower and nuzzled the back of Raphael's neck. One hand reached out and twisted the handle to force the water back to jaguar-preferred temperatures.

"Who said you were invited?" Sinking teeth into his lower lip, Raphael managed to hold in the moan of pleasure as Sebastian's warm body leaned against his, arms wrapped around him.

"Stop complaining. We both know you don't mean it. You know I'll never keep the answer from you. Just believe in me. I have everything planned to bring Hillary into our lives forever. A way that doesn't rely on the sporadic chance of the dance," Sebastian said, nibbling and kissing along the sensitive line of Raphael's neck and shoulder.

Unable to deny his lover, Raphael leaned to the side, closing his eyes in pleasure. Moans escaped him while Sebastian's hands moved over his chest. Nimble fingers threaded through dark chest hair, plucked and flicked the curls. They then found the dark, flat nipples against the pectorals. Rubbing and gently pinching until they hardened, until Raphael moaned, arching against his lover's body, one arm wrapped around Sebastian's head, fingers threaded through blond hair, gripping hard.

When Raphael turned his head to plea for more, Sebastian captured his lips before he spoke the words. They knew each other too well, too long for words. Opening his mouth for his lover's tongue, Raphael groaned into Sebastian's mouth when his lover's hands went further down his belly, tracing the lines of his abdomen. He tried not to laugh when those fingers hit the ticklish side of his stomach, just above his left hip. His fingers tightened in Sebastian's hair in a warning to stop playing and love him. He wanted hot, hard, sex. He wanted the shower stall and mirrors to steam from their love and not the water temperature.

Breaking the kiss, Raphael savored this time with his lover, fingers moving over his smooth skin, tracing over his sleek flank muscles, slanting toward his expectant groin. His erection hot and full, tilted against his belly, tip coated with cream.

"Touch me, *por favor*," Raphael groaned.

"Do you want me to touch you?" Sebastian teased, leaning to the side, nipping at Sebastian's ear.

Reaching a hand back, Raphael gripped Sebastian's erection. "Do you want this?"

"Bastard," Sebastian growled, dropping his hand, and echoed Raphael's grip.

Raphael groaned when calloused fingers gripped his hard cock. He arched his back, leaning against his lover. Those fingers knew him so well, yet they opened and closed against him in varying motions. Nails and tips trailed up and down, measured, circled his girth, and followed the path of the engorged blood vessels that throbbed under the silky skin.

"Damn, Bastian," he moaned, head turned restlessly against his lover's shoulder.

Then his lover took him in a good hard grip and began that rhythmic push, pull, up, down motion full of friction. It was full of sex and the motion of pure fucking. Then his lover upped things to another sensational level. Sebastian cupped his heavy sac of testicles and rubbed and rolled them against one another until Raphael cried out.

He rode the edge of need, rocked back and forth, from heels to the balls of his feet. Hips thrust against Bastian's hands. His fingers held on to Bastian's hair and hip in tight grips. Breathing became harder with every surge of that palm. The shower beat down on them, adding to the sensitivity his lover built across his body.

He cried out when Bastian sank his teeth into his shoulder, knowing he needed the fierceness to go over the edge. He felt his sac tighten. Something inside him pushed him over. Hot streams of seed jettisoned from his penis, coating his belly, Sebastian's fingers, and the tiles before the shower washed it all away. He continued to come hard until his balls ached and his body drooped against his lover's embrace.

* * * *

"Trying to kill me or just distract me?" Raphael managed to say when he got his mind and mouth under control.

Sebastian chuckled while his hands poured and massaged the shampoo through Raphael's dark curls. "A little of both, love. Did you enjoy?"

"Always, when I'm in your arms," Raphael said, moaning as his scalp got some attention. Until he was pushed under the deluge to rinse. Sputtering, spitting out water and suds, he cracked open an eye. He jammed an elbow into Sebastian's gut.

"Damn, I love you," Sebastian said after getting his breath back. He snagged Raphael, leaned him back, and planted a long hot kiss on his lips.

"*Te quiero*," Raphael murmured.

After more water play that outlasted the size of their water heater, they dropped on the oversize bed, wet than dry. Curled in each other's arms, snuggling, playful, loving, lips touched, nuzzled, nipped, kissed. Long legs tangled under the crisp cotton sheets.

Lifting Raphael's hand, Sebastian matched his fingers to his partners'. He then studied the lines and play of colors and calluses on the palm. Soon he interlinked their fingers and held them against his chest where his heart beat.

"Sebastian?"

Grumbling about the impatience of his Latin lover, Sebastian dropped their joined hands on his chest. He met Raphael's searching gaze. "Courtship."

"What?"

"We will court our Hillary."

"What will that do to bring her into our lives?"

"It's the way I found to love and mate with Hillary without anyone taking her from us."

"When did you start looking?"

"When we first spotted her at the clan meeting, the first time the High Alpha introduced her as a new transfer from her father's clan. How beautiful she looked, so nervous and timid, but a spark lingered in her eyes, in her body. We both saw it around her."

"That drab dress did nothing to flatter her curvy body and thick curls, yet she managed to stand out."

"Most likely her father's doing."

"Where did you find this courtship idea?"

"In the library. It's written in the laws, but it's been forgotten over time. Most only remember the dances. There is another way to find a mate without the dances. One where we can choose our own mates, if there happens to be interest amongst a pair of kin, instead of waiting for the dance."

"Courtship?"

Sebastian bobbed his head against Raphael's cheek and neck. "Old-fashioned courtship. It happens over the course of time before the seasonal dance. We have less than a week till the moon."

"How do we do this?"

"We set up an announcement in front of some members of the clan of our intent to court her before the dance, like at her office. That begins the process and hopefully it will be done in front of the bitch."

Raphael looked up to see Sebastian's satisfied smile. "When do we begin?"

"Tomorrow."

Chapter 5

Dry mouth, achy head, Hillary felt miserable the next day, stuck in her cubicle in the IT department trying to decode bugs in a new accounting program. Four cups of strong coffee, a couple of prescription-strength aspirin, a fully loaded breakfast, and there still wasn't relief. It definitely put her off the idea of another whiskey binge. Then there were the dreams haunting her all night.

Passionate, sensual dreams.

A rush of liquid need dropped into her lower body, dampening her panties. Her thighs tightened. She crossed her legs to try to hide the scent of her sudden arousal from any kin males in the surrounding cubicles.

As soon as she rushed home after leaving two sublime men who desired her above all others on the bar's floor, she had stripped and dropped on the bed, hoping to fall into a blissful, drunken sleep. Instead, she dreamt of them. Of their gentle attention, seduction, hands, lips, bodies, warmth, and loving devotion to her. Lust versus rules. She felt torn between the difficult options. A moan left her as she dropped her head on the desk.

"Aww, is your head hurting? I heard you went on a bender last night while Josh spent the night with me. I told you not to try to play with the big girls. You'll only get burned," Belinda Alcott said in a chastising tone while her girlfriends snickered and jeered.

Underneath the desk, one of Hillary's hands fisted, ready to punch the female's lights out in front of everyone who worked in the IT department. Calming her body and mind, she looked up and met her evil counterpart's proud expression.

"Did you come all the way down to IT to gloat, Belinda? I thought you did enough of that when you fucked Josh at the meeting," Hillary said, rising out of her chair. Her clenched fist moved behind her back, staying out of sight while it flexed. She noticed the others within the department, including her boss, watched their interaction.

"I claimed my mate before you tried to step into a position that wasn't yours. It seems you still don't know your place." Belinda stepped into Hillary's personal space.

"Oh, I know my place very well, thanks to kin like you and your kind. You don't stop for a moment telling me where my place is. The newcomer kept at the bottom of the clan, worthless to everyone and anyone, especially to all the kin males. Pushed and kicked, until you make sure the poor cat has no conscience, strength, or positive sense of self. Just the way you prefer your cats. Do I have that right?" Hillary crossed arms under her not-so-endowed bosom and stared at the stronger female. "How many others fell for your tricks and games, Belinda? How many suckers did you play so you could feel better about yourself?"

"You little bitch," Belinda snapped.

"Don't even think of hitting her. Not after the bullshit you pulled at the meeting," Marcus called, stepping behind Hillary's back to support her.

"She back talked me, her superior!"

"I don't give a shit."

"How dare—"

"I dare more than you can even think or say. Nor can you run and complain to Daddy about me. He can't stop me or counteract my decisions. I rule here," Marcus snapped.

"I can still make life hell for her."

"Try it and you'll regret it."

"Marcus, please," Hillary said, placing a hand on his arm.

"Oh, now you're trying to protect your boss? Don't think you can hide behind him forever, little brat," Belinda said.

"Don't think I'll stay in this position where you'll be able to make those threats," Hillary said.

"I'm your superior."

Hillary snorted.

"With your attitude, you're no one's superior. You damn well deserved my sneer and more of the same," Marcus said. "In no way do your attempts of snobbery mean Hillary deserves punishment for whatever excuse or fault you make up in the pathetic gray matter you call a brain."

"Excuse me, I have a delivery," a young man called out, stepping forward with a huge flower arrangement in his hands.

"Oooooh! Look what my Josh-kitty sent me!" Belinda cooed.

"Delivered to our floor?" Marcus asked.

"Everyone knows I came down here. Come with me to my floor," Belinda said, heading toward the young man to take him back to the elevator.

"Wait a minute," Marcus said, putting a hand on her arm to stop her, and turned to the young man. "Please ignore her interruptions. She has no business on this floor."

"Uhh, sure, sir," the man said, looking back and forth.

"Now, who is the name on the delivery?"

"Hillary Kearney."

Hillary blinked twice and then winced when Belinda started to screech.

"And the floor?"

"According to the papers, I'm supposed to be on this floor," the young man said, glancing at the card in his fingers.

"*What?*"

The delivery boy stepped back from the screeching, stacked blonde. "Umm, do I have the right floor and lady?"

"You do." Marcus pointed to Hillary. "They go to her."

"Me? They're for me." Hillary grinned at Belinda and her friends.

"Who would send you flowers like this?" Belinda demanded, slamming hands on hips. "No male would send a newcomer flowers. You're banned from speaking or touching another until Friday's season."

"That's for me to find out and you to simmer about until Friday, Belinda," Hillary answered and smiled at the deliveryman. "You can put it over here. Oh, they're absolutely stunning." She pointed to her desk, moving out of the way.

"Oh, good, it's a little heavy. The gentlemen asked for the largest arrangement possible and were very specific about these types of flowers when they were ordering. It amused our florist to no end, had her chuckling for hours while she raced around to find them in time for the delivery," the man said with a grin.

"Gentlemen?"

"Yes, ma'am, there were two names on the order."

At that, Hillary knew who had sent the flowers and stared at them. She couldn't believe they would go through all this trouble for her, especially after how she ran away from them. Could they really mean what they told her about choosing her as their third mate?

"Why were they so specific about these flowers?"

"It was something about being a specific color to match their idea and preference."

"Oh?"

"It gets much better, miss."

"How so?"

"Then the two men fought over the message on the card. I waited about fifteen minutes while they went through about five drafts."

"Fifteen minutes to wait for drafts of a card?" Hillary chuckled at the idea of Sebastian and Raphael fighting over a pen. She couldn't think of them arguing something simple as putting words down on a piece of paper.

"Two men? How could it be two men who sent one vase?" Belinda interrupted and tried to push past Marcus, who held out an arm to keep her from entering Hillary's space after the young man set the bouquet down and handed Hillary the large card. She glared at Marcus, who shook his head and didn't budge a muscle.

The young man nodded. "Yup, it was two guys. Before I leave, I need you to sign here for me, miss, to acknowledge the delivery." He stuck an electronic board and pen toward Hillary, who signed her name. "Thank you much. Enjoy the flowers."

"I will. What woman couldn't enjoy such exquisite things. Do I owe anything?" She ran a finger over the corner of the card and stared at the flamboyant flowers.

"No, the gentlemen took care of everything, even added a generous tip for me. You must be something special."

She blushed at that.

"Bye," he said and walked away.

Hillary sat in her chair after taking a deep sniff of the delicious bouquet of Vendela Ivory roses and Baby Blue Eyes wildflowers. The florist combined them with stems of limonium and clusters of beargrass in the extra large, premium, black art-glass vase. Raising a hand, she let her fingers grace the velvet-soft petals of the sumptuous roses. Never in her life had she received such an enormous bouquet. She opened the envelope and card.

Vendela Ivory roses don't dare to compare to the perfection of your skin. Baby Blue Eyes wildflowers shy from the natural color of your eyes. Black art-glass is dull against the shine of your hair. Yet this is all Nature could give us to compare to the beauty of you, our beloved Hillary.

We ask for permission to court you until the Fire Moon Dance, where we will dance and be mated under the full moon in front of the entire clan. Our Fire Moon Goddess will bless our union and give us all we seek together.

For it is you, our sweet jaguar, we choose for our triad. You and no other kin female.

Please say yes and accept us into your life and heart.
Sincerely yours, Sebastian and Raphael.

Blushing after reading the words, she fluttered the card like a fan as a smile curled her lips. She laughed and leaned back in the chair before she spun around like a child.

"What the hell? Who the hell sent you those flowers? How dare an unmated tom, let alone two of them, go against the laws to send flowers to a female? They didn't participate in a dance," Belinda demanded, trying to ruin Hillary's happiness.

"That is none of your business. I believe it's time for you and your friends to return to your offices and work," Marcus said, stepped in front of them, pushed out his energy.

"Someone will find out and put a stop to it. This can't happen, not with a newcomer!"

Hillary rose and smiled, a force to reckon with now she had someone, two divine males, who cared for her. "Not everyone in the kin thinks like you, Belinda. You shall find out soon enough."

"Little bitch cat," she sneered.

"I wouldn't say that aloud. Someone could think you're talking about yourself," Hillary replied with a grin as she turned and sat, and sniffed the Vendela roses.

A screech and hiss left Belinda as she flounced to the elevator. Her friends followed, surrounding and protecting her with words and gestures.

None of it entered Hillary's bubble of happiness.

* * * *

A couple of hours later, the bubble increased when a different deliveryman appeared at her desk with another package. This time the bag came from a popular jewelry store just outside the clan's territory. All the kin females in the IT department oohed at the sight and gathered around Hillary's desk as she pulled out the large box. She plucked off the sinful satin ribbon and pulled out the inner box.

Nibbling on her lower lip, she lifted the lid. Her lower jaw dropped. The jewels appeared before them, nestled against the ivory satin bedding.

"Oh my goodness," she whispered at the sight of the glorious diamond and sapphire necklace and earring set sparkling, glistening.

"Oh, Hillary, those are stunning. Whose attention did you catch at the meeting?" a lady asked.

"It seems two mysterious kin males. Who are they? Who are these handsome admirers spending a fortune on you?" another asked in a teasing tone. "I never saw Belinda so jealous of another kin female before. It was fantastic to watch someone get one over her."

"Oh yes, way to get one on her, Hillary."

Hillary blushed as she stared at the jewels and plucked the card from the bag. She flipped it open to read the note.

We hope these come close to the sparkles our Goddess created in your eyes. We hope to see those gorgeous sparkles tonight.
Yours, S & R.

"Well?"

Hillary nibbled on her lower lip and shook her head. "Not until the Fire Moon Dance."

"Or until we see them courting you. It's obvious they're courting you the old-fashioned way. That's the way it used to be, and then it was finalized at the Fire Moon Dance."

"Courting?"

Valerie smiled. "You young folks don't know the old ways, but these gentlemen found the old laws. Now, they are using them to declare their interest in you."

Hillary looked at the older kin female, Valerie. "Is that true? How does the courtship work?"

Val nodded. "I wish it remained that way instead of a young female being forced to flit from one male to the next every season. It's too harsh. The males should court you young ladies, treat all of you as the ladies you are. Only then should you choose to bed the male, if you wish, after the dance, if there's a connection felt during the courting process. Looks like your beaus are returning to the old ways. They put in their declaration to court you with the flowers and jewelry. Good for them. Good for you, honey." Squeezing Hillary's shoulder in support, she went back to her desk, shooing the others away.

After admiring the jewels again, Hillary closed the box and placed it back in the bag. She set it near the vase. Her heart raced with thoughts of what her courting males would do next. Then it skipped and fluttered as a panic attack hit her. Hard.

She pressed a hand to her chest. Her breathing changed. Sweat gathered at her forehead.

Her father. Her father would not be pleased at this courtship. At this change in his plans. He didn't like when someone altered his plans without his permission.

Turning from the monitors, she pressed a fist to her lips as she tried to get her breathing under control. Her eyes closed tight as the shouts of her father rang through her head. How she had memorized his shouting, the beatings she took whenever his displeasure rose. He sent her here for a specific purpose, to unite the clans with a mating. Only Josh wasn't free anymore. How could she tell her father she had failed? How could she tell him about Raphael and Sebastian?

She wanted the chance to see how this courtship worked. She loved the feeling that rushed through her at the sight of the flowers and the jewelry. Concentrating on that sensation, she pushed back the harsh thought of her father. She hummed with pleasure as she worked through the difficult tangle of code and bugs to get the new program working.

* * * *

A little later, Marcus walked over to her desk, a funny smile on his face. He leaned against one wall and watched her untangle a bug and demolish it. "How is the accounting program coming along?"

"Slowly, but it's moving. It should be ready for testing by next week. By the way, Marcus, I apologize for earlier—" she started, but he held up a hand.

"It wasn't your fault. That issue rests entirely on her shoulders. You're new and someone should have warned you about her. It's high time someone needs to put a stop to her shenanigans before it goes too far and causes more problems. Now, on to far better things," he said with a smile.

"Better things?" She turned in her chair.

"Are you at a stopping point?"

She nodded.

"Good. As your superior in the clan, I've been informed by your gentlemen callers of their request to court you over the next week."

"Oh? And?"

"I've gladly given then my full approval. I approve of this match."

She blushed. Her heart skipped a beat while her breathing quickened.

"Now. Collect your things and that charming little jewelry bag. Your gentlemen courters called me and requested I release you early this evening. They set up some arrangements that require your attention and appearance," Marcus said.

"They did what?"

"You're first to go to Shayla's Salon, where she will take care of your hair and makeup. Then you are to hurry home."

"My home?"

Marcus nodded. "A chosen outfit is waiting for you to wear for an evening out, along with your gift. They will pick you up at six o'clock sharp."

"Oh my," Hillary said, blushing at the details as she gathered her purse and the jewelry bag. She brushed her fingers over the delicate petals. "I don't want to leave them here. I don't want her to go near them."

"She'll never touch them," Valerie said.

"Thanks, Val," Hillary said.

"Leave them here. I'm sure your courters will be indulging you with many more flowers until the night of the Fire Moon Dance. Now, go, hurry on to Shayla's," Marcus said with a laugh.

"Go, honey, and have fun!" Valerie called out over the cubicle while others called out their own encouragements and shouts of laughter and joy.

Laughing, Hillary waved to her office mates and raced away to the elevator, digging for her keys.

Chapter 6

After the salon thoroughly pampered her from head to toe, Hillary slid out of her car and moved to the single floor townhome given to her upon acceptance by the clan. Part of the initial agreement set between her father and the elders, she fell in love with the home at first sight. She stopped and stared at what now graced her door.

Tied to the knocker was a bright red bow with a Vendela Ivory rose and a card. She plucked it off the door and opened the card to read the message.

Hope you enjoy your afternoon of beauty, though it could only enhance what nature gave you to begin with. Please don't be alarmed. We got the key to your door to help with this surprise and many more to come. Your outfit waits in your bedroom. Can't wait to see you this evening.

Leave the door unlocked. We'll find our way to you.

Yours truly, S & R.

Shaking her head at the lengths Sebastian and Raphael went to in order to make sure everything happened for this special day, she slipped her key in the lock and opened the door. She stared at the ivory and blue petals strewn across the wood floor leading to the back bedroom. Closing the door, she tossed her purse on the loveseat and followed the path to find more petals scattered on the bed where a wispy satin and lacy lingerie set waited. A gorgeous, frothy concoction of an empire dress in royal blue hung from the closet door.

Kicking off her work shoes, she went to the closet to look at the provocative gown and saw the strappy heels resting on the floor. She couldn't believe they went shopping for her and picked all this out. Rushing back to her bureau, she set the jewelry bag down and dug into a drawer for her secret weapon to battle the slight bulge of her lower body half. She found the nude-colored body shaper that would help suck in the extra pounds and flab she battled to lose. If she wanted to do the lingerie and dress any justice, she must wear the dreaded shapewear.

"Okay, the battle to pull them on begins," she swore, sat on the edge of the bed, and stripped off her work clothes.

While she huffed, puffed, wiggled, groaned, tugged, and heaved, she lost complete and total track of time. Soon, she finally stood up and stretched the body shaper into place under her B-cup breasts. Patting her now flat tummy and somewhat shapely hips, she moved to the full-length mirror and checked out her image.

"Not bad, Kearney, not bad. Lost about ten pounds wiggling into this monster," she told her image. She checked the clock.

Twenty minutes left.

"Ah, crap! Now I have to scramble!"

Snatching up a few tissues, she pressed them against her neck and chest to wipe away the sweat. She then pressed a clean one against her face, careful of the delicate makeup application. Sitting on the bed, she applied her favorite scented body lotion and then a generous few sprays of matching perfume at her pulse points.

Reaching out, she slipped on the lingerie. Shifting and plumping her breasts to create some hint of a décolletage, she stood in front of the mirror.

"About as good as you're gonna get, girlfriend."

Turning to the dress, she did a little wiggle of glee at the beauty of the garment. She had never worn anything so glorious, not even from her father. Unlike Belinda's, her father never doted on her or spoiled her with frivolities. She worked for everything she earned, including his love and admiration. It became the reason why she accepted the transfer her father had set up with this new clan to come here.

Would she ruin everything she worked for by accepting this courtship with Sebastian and Raphael? Would she lose her father's love if she failed to become a member of this prestigious clan? She wanted to do everything he asked her, but what if this path with Sebastian and Raphael was correct. If what her heart needed and wasn't what her father demanded from her, could she be strong enough to stand against him?

Whimpering, Hillary dropped her hands from the dress and stepped back. Hugging arms around her waist, she pulled in a few deep breaths. After the earlier panic attack, she didn't want to deal with another one. They were getting far more frequent again, just like when she was home, around him. Would she ever be free?

Shaking her head hard, she moved back, unzipped the dress, slipped off the full straps, and slid it off the padded hanger. Lowering it to the floor, she stepped into the opening, and lifted the dress in place. Reaching behind, she zipped the empire bodice after tugging up the straps. She made sure the straps covered the bra straps and caressed her fingers over the edge of the scoop-neck bodice.

With a chuckle, she twirled and twisted in front of the mirror. The full skirt furled and flared around her knees in a delicious, flirty way.

There was a warning knock on her front door, disturbing her twirling.

"Hillary? It's Sebastian and Raphael," Sebastian called out, his strong tone echoing through her home.

"Are you decent?" Raphael's sultry Latino accent added, causing her to chuckle.

"If not, we are more than willing to help."

Laughing harder at their playful antics, Hillary scooped up the sparkly shoes, purse, and jewelry bag. She hurried down the hall before the males could enter the bedroom. She slowed when she caught sight of the absolutely decadent sight appearing in her living room.

Looking between the men, she admired their handsome evening attire. They were both in dark suits. Sebastian's had a light pinstripe effect, while Raphael's had a shine to the fabric. To highlight his unusual eyes, Sebastian paired his suit with a mint green shirt and left the top buttons open. Raphael kept his simple with a cream shirt and a matching thin, dark tie, perfectly knotted.

"You two look wonderful."

Turning to face her, Sebastian clasped his hands behind his back and nodded his head in a respectful fashion. "Thank you, darling Hillary. You look divine in the dress. Hmm, Raphael, you were right about the color. She does look superb. I was wrong to ever doubt you."

Raphael chuckled as he moved toward Hillary. "*Buenas noches*, Hillary." He dropped his head and took a deep sniff from her neck. "You look beautiful, smell delectable. What is your perfume?"

"Sum…Summertime Hill. A special blend," she whispered, lifting her head to stare into his dark gaze when he raised his head from her neck.

"Suits you. Just like this sapphire, brings out the blue," he said, crooking a finger under her chin. "I hope you enjoy your presents. We had a wonderful time choosing them." Leaning in, he kissed her cheek. It was gentle and respectful, a courtship kiss.

"Hmm, I heard about the interesting time you two had with the flowers," she said, blushing and looking between them. "You gave the florist and her staff quite a laugh. The delivery boy couldn't stop talking about it while he dropped off the flowers. My office couldn't stop talking about it after he left."

"Really? What did he have to say?" Raphael asked.

"How the flowers had to be an exact color, the arrangement the right size, you went through about five drafts for the card, and made him wait over fifteen minutes. I believe you went a little overdramatic, gentlemen. Don't you think?"

"I told you there would be a ruckus with those flowers," Sebastian said, nudging his partner with an elbow in the ribs.

"You insist on perfection. I wanted to make sure it was there with the flowers," Raphael said in a calm fashion that had them all laughing.

"The flowers were beautiful as well as the message. Then the jewels arrived. I never saw such a fabulous set of jewelry in my life. It's a magnificent set."

"I know they will be beautiful adorning your neck and ears, *querida*," Raphael said, tracing a finger against her collarbone. "Now, where is your jewelry?"

She held up the bag.

"Ah, there we go, completing the ensemble." Raphael took the bag, plucked the box, and tossed the bag to Sebastian, who caught it. He opened the box and removed the delicate jewelry from their satin bedding. He underhanded the box to his partner, who placed it back in the bag and on the coffee table.

Sebastian then came forward and took the heels and purse from Hillary's trembling hands before she could say anything. He pressed a gentle kiss to her cheek at the same time. After a soft nuzzle with his nose behind her ear, bringing a chuckle to her lips, he settled on the loveseat. He set her everyday purse on the coffee table and opened it.

"Sebastian, what are you doing with my purse?" She watched Raphael manipulate the delicate clasp of one earring before sliding a lock of hair behind her ear.

He turned to gaze at her with a somewhat innocent smile filled with devilish delight. "I'm only going to transfer the necessary items to your evening purse. It's what you were going to do, correct?"

"Yes, after Raphael helps with my jewelry." She held still while Raphael slid the first earring through, closed the clasp and repeated the motion with the matching earring. She lifted her gaze to stare into his chocolate gaze as he stood in front of her, the front of his suit brushing her skirt.

Grinning, Raphael leaned over, nuzzled noses. He then held the necklace in his hands and undid the lobster clasp. While he seemed to take a long time in placing it around her neck, she watched Sebastian open her wallet, pluck out only her identification, and set it in the tiny purse. There wasn't much room in the tiny clasp clutch.

"I need more than my ID card."

"We're taking care of everything tonight."

"Please, as a precaution. Something my father forced into my teaching no matter what happens." She noticed how they looked between each other.

"Always rely on yourself?" Sebastian asked.

She bobbed her head and shrugged. "It worked for me. Please do as I ask or the night ends here."

"What else would you like?"

She listed, "My Visa card, cash, cell phone, and my house key. The rest can stay in the purse and unseen by prying male eyes. Understand?"

Sebastian grinned and silently transferred exactly what she said. He rose to where she had set her keys and pulled off the single ring to place inside the clutch. "Anything else, my dear?"

She shook her head. "No, thank you."

Raphael finished with the necklace and positioned the pendant above her décolletage. He stepped back and nodded. He dropped to his knees in front of her.

"Raphael?"

"Place your hands on my shoulders. I will help with your shoes. Bastian, the heels, if you please?" Raphael held out one hand while sliding another down Hillary's calf.

Moaning in pleasure at the gentle touch, Hillary did as he asked. She let him lift one foot, slip it in the glittery shoe, then fix the delicate clasp around her ankle. He helped her balance on the heel and then shift before he lifted her other foot. After another caress of his hand, he placed her foot down.

She nibbled on her lower lip while watching Raphael's careful motion. He then rose with a smile, Sebastian coming to stand next to him, handing over her clutch. Somehow, he also pulled a boutonniere type of arrangement of a Vendela Ivory rose and Baby Blue wildflower with a bit of the grass from his inner pocket. Plumping the rosebud with his fingers, fixing the delicate petals, he plucked something from the back.

"Is it ruined? I told you we should have brought the box for it, as well as wrapped a wet towel around the base to keep the flowers moist and fresh." Raphael turned, almost straining to make sure to check.

"Would you relax?"

Raphael hissed, baring a set of sharp feline fangs.

"Oh drop the fangs, tom cat, and chill." Sebastian waved him away.

Watching their interaction, Hillary hid a smile and tried to smother a chuckle.

"Nothing is ruined. It's perfectly fine, fabulous in fact. Just as I told you the flowers would be to match the dress." Sebastian stepped closer, lifted a few curls to the side, and pinned the hair flower piece in place with bobby pins. "There, now that completes the look. I knew the flowers would be stunning against your hair color." He rearranged the curls to match the rest of the hairdo Shalya created. "See, Raphael, I told you they were the perfect touch."

"*Sí, sí*, you were right," Raphael said.

Smiling, now almost shy under the scrutinizing looks of the males, Hillary waited for their approvals. Instead, she saw pleasure, admiration, and lust in their eyes. All for her. "Now what?"

They held out their elbows, bowing in the elegant, courtly manner.

Sebastian grinned and said, "Now comes the best part. We shall show you an evening out with us as your escorts."

Chapter 7

After a trip in the stretch white limousine, settled between her escorts, Hillary entered the elegant four-star restaurant on the edge of the clan territory and human city, Dove Star. It was a blended cuisine restaurant and one she had always wanted to go and try, but could never afford. It was something the scum had often suggested just after their dance, but they never came through with the promise.

Now she walked through the double doors on the arms of her dual escorts, the most handsome of the entire clan. She was dressed in finery from head to toe and pampered at the clan's finest salon.

"Gentlemen, lady, welcome to Dove Star. Do you have a reservation this evening?" the tuxedo-clad maître d' asked, looking up from the cherry wood platform where he conducted his business.

"We do. The name is Salazar," Raphael said. "Table for three."

"Oh yes, our finest table is reserved for you, sirs, ma'am," the man said with a wider smile than even before. He picked up three leather-bound menus and guided them through the restaurant's floor.

Along the way, they passed the table where Joshua held Belinda's arm, trying to keep her in her chair. They all saw her face red, fuming with the desire to rise and scream when she realized who sent Hillary the flowers earlier.

Sebastian sidled closer to Hillary, wrapping his arm more firmly around her waist. His fingers spread out across her hip. He leaned down and whispered, "You'll never need to fear her. Soon she'll have no power over any of us."

Turning away from the angry she-cat, Hillary nodded and glanced up at the tall, blond kin who chose her. She graced him with a warm smile. "Unfortunately, she'll turn her claws onto her next victim."

"I hope her reputation is damaged to the point where it stops her. She's done enough to this clan," he said and nuzzled her cheek.

"Enough about her, she has no place at this table," Raphael whispered.

Reaching the table, Raphael shook his head and stepped behind Hillary's chair. He pulled it from the table and held out a hand. He helped her sit down and pushed the chair in for her. His hands graced her shoulders and neck before he leaned down to place a kiss for all kin to see on her nape.

"Enjoying your night out?" he asked, settling in the chair next to her.

"You two are creating quite the show for everyone," she said, noticing the arrangement placed them in a way so that all the diners could watch their every movement and interaction.

"It's exactly what we wish. We must declare our intent to court you in front of the clan," Sebastian said, taking his own chair.

"You did that at my office."

"The High Alpha and some other Elders are here for dinner," Sebastian said.

"We're taking no chances with our declaration," Raphael added.

"Why?"

The men turned to her and each took a hand in theirs.

"Mates, Hillary. You are our mate, our *pareja*. Simple as that," Raphael said.

"But you're already mated, to each other," she said. "It's impossible to have a third."

"Not impossible. It's rare, but not impossible. It's been known to happen before, but rarely spoken about, like courtship midseason when a dance match doesn't work," Sebastian confirmed.

"You believe I'm your third mate?"

"Not believe. We know," Sebastian said. "Scent, energy, emotions, though only the dance will tell for sure."

"And sex," she whispered.

Raphael laughed aloud and pressed a kiss to her trembling fingers. "Oh yes indeed, that will tell us for sure whether we are the truest of mates. Though, we have no doubt about you."

"What if there is a doubt?"

"There is none."

"You don't know that until it happens, under the moon, in front of everyone. There could be a doubt. What happens to me? I could be blackballed, returned to my clan, shunned, proclaimed a whore or worse."

They leaned closer and stared at her.

"We would never let that happen. There is no doubt in our minds. If there was, we wouldn't begin the courtship." Raphael reached out, cupped her chin, and drew her complete attention to him.

"Then why don't I feel all of this?"

"You're scared of the consequences. You felt it last night at the bar."

"It was the alcohol."

"It let you relax under all the pressure on your shoulders. You desire us, both of us. You have since the first meeting you attended. Do you dream of us? Of being with us?" Raphael leaned close, whispered in her ear.

Her eyes closed as he whispered scintillating details of what they wanted to do to her, with her in the night, in bed, out of bed, all around their home. Cream filled her shapewear. Her nipples tightened into taut buds against the silk of the new bra.

"Yes," she moaned.

"Every night?" Sebastian whispered in her other ear.

"Yes."

His fingertip traced the outer edge of her ear. "That's the first step of mating, the sensual, erotic dreams. It is our minds, our energy reaching for one another, letting us know we found our match. You dream of both of us?"

"Yes."

"You match us both, like we match you and each other."

"Why shouldn't we all enjoy one another? Who should make all the rules and tell us this is wrong? They are not living our lives, not a part of this relationship. They are not in our bed. We say this is right for us. You are right for us," Raphael insisted.

"You do wish to be right for us," Sebastian said, moving his hand up her thigh.

"Yes. Yes, I wish it."

"Then there is nothing wrong with what we do."

Hillary licked her lips and moaned. She squirmed in the chair and repositioned her legs as more heat flooded her legs. Her clit hardened and throbbed. She wanted to stick her hand between her legs and rub the swollen nub to give herself some relief.

"Uh-uh, no touching yourself unless we say so," Sebastian said, capturing her hand and kissing her fingers.

"Is she trying to do what I think?" Raphael teased.

Heat flooded her cheeks.

"I believe so. I believe our little talk and touching heated up our kitty's body so much she wants some relief."

"Well now, I'm impressed, *mi dulce*. So much *pasíon* riding inside you," Raphael said, letting the Spanish accent roll over his words, a purr coming forward.

More heat flooded her cheeks while her inner petals pulsed.

"Pardon me? Welcome to Dove Star. I'm your waiter for the evening," the young man said with a brilliant white smile, wearing a black and white outfit with an apron around his waist.

Relieved at the distraction of the waiter, Hillary leaned back in her chair as the males sat back. She tried to calm her body and listen to the waiter's spiel about the evening's specials, the wine list, and a variety of other things. Hearing something about a grilled mahi-mahi dish, she ordered it while the men ordered thick steaks, rare, with a light wine and a couple other courses to complete an appetizer, a salad course, and dinner.

Once the waiter left then returned with a simple plate of tapas, bread, and dipping sauces, with water and wine to fill their glasses, Hillary felt her heart skip a beat when her males—for indeed they were her males—leaned closer to her.

"Good evening. Raphael? Sebastian?" their High Alpha asked, ignoring her position between them.

Hillary dropped her eyes out of respect for Irvine Thurston's position and felt a light sense of anger from her males at how the alpha ignored her presence. She heard their chairs move and knew they rose to bow their heads before sitting. Both of them immediately took hold of her hands.

"High Alpha Thurston, do you know Hillary Kearney?" Sebastian asked.

"Why are you with this newcomer? No other is to touch her until the next seasonal dance. She is partnered to Joshua for the duration regardless of his mating to Belinda, the rules still stand and are not to be broken," the older jaguar asked, not wanting to go through the introductions.

"No one will touch but us, High Alpha. We put in a claim of courtship this morning," Sebastian said.

"The both of you?"

"Yes, sir, we will be a triad if the Fire Moon Goddess accepts and blesses our binding during the dance."

"I will need to discuss this with the Elders. This is unusual, Sebastian."

"There is no discussion, sir. The courtship of a potential mate is written in the laws for anyone to locate. There is no need for approval by the Elders, only the Fire Moon Goddess. We answer only to her, as do all the jaguars in terms of mating. We put our claim of courtship in writing and proclaimed it at Hillary's office by way of a flower delivery. This evening we certify the claim in person." Sebastian kissed her fingers.

Lifting her gaze from the table, Hillary stared at Sebastian and gave him a tremulous smile. When Raphael reciprocated the kiss, she swiveled to present him the same smile.

"You intend to go forward with this claim? With or without the council's ruling?"

"To the end, sir," Sebastian said.

"To the end with our mates," Raphael echoed. "As Sebastian said, only the Goddess can bless our union, not the council."

"Young lady?" the alpha asked. "What say you?"

"I accept their claim of courtship and pray the Goddess honors us with her blessing," Hillary said, meeting the High Alpha's gaze.

"No matter your father's wishes and distinct desires when he presented your request to join this clan? This goes against the request."

"I live my life under the ways of the Goddess, not his, sir," she said. "The womb he bargained with belongs to me, not him."

"You would take such a risk against your father for these toms you barely know?"

"My heart knows them. My dreams know them. My jaguar will know them soon. So I will know them. After the dance and our Goddess's blessing, I will love them."

"Very well, I warn you. Though I send updates to your father, I perceive he already knows in one form or another. I would put nothing past your father."

"Do what you believe you must, sir." Her stomach soured as thoughts roiled what her father would think of her choice, of her going against the rules.

"Enjoy your meal," High Alpha Thurston said, returning to his table.

Tugging her hands from her males, placing them on her lap, Hillary blinked hard, pushed back the tears. She chomped hard on her inner cheek, held onto the new pain to stop the old, harsh memories that rose from the alpha's words, her father's words.

One warm hand went to her thigh while another settled on her shoulder. From the simple touch, she could tell the difference between their hands.

"What was that all about?" Raphael asked, leaning closer.

"Transfer business. It is nothing, really, petty and stupid," she said in a tight tone.

"Do we need to speak with your father about our intentions?" Sebastian asked.

"*No!*" It escaped louder than she wanted.

Others in the restaurant turned and stared at their table.

"Hillary?" Sebastian rubbed a hand over her shoulder.

"No, Sebastian, there is no need. I will speak with him."

"As one tom to another, it should be our duty," Raphael said.

"Really, there is no need." Blinking hard, she pasted a fake smile on her lips and turned to each of them. "Let us enjoy our evening. Please."

"But—"

She pressed her fingers to Raphael's lips, then to Sebastian's when he tried to say something, and shook her head. "Let us enjoy our evening, for it would only spoil everything from the mood to the food. I don't want that."

"Hillary," Sebastian tried.

She shook her head again. "Please?"

Tears glazed her eyes until the men agreed.

Chapter 8

Memories of the wonderful night, in spite of the High Alpha's interruption and the reminder that her father's upcoming wrath would rain upon her when he found out what she was doing, filled her mind as Hillary slowly woke the next morning. Snuggling into the pillows, she curled on her side to see the delicate flower piece she wore in her hair resting on the nightstand. She reached out and touched the soft petal with one fingertip.

All the touches, the smiles, their laughter and joy from being with her rushed to the forefront and it thrilled her to no end. These two powerful alpha toms and guardians of the clan chose her above all the other possibilities to become their mate. A unique triad. Almost unheard of among the clan's lore, but here she was, about to become a part of one when the full rising of the fire moon signaled their mating dance.

Until then, her toms cherished and courted her like a gentle lady of olden times. At the door last night, they kissed and hugged her in turn. Raphael opened the door for her and then made sure all was safe within her home before they let her cross the threshold. After another series of kisses and hugs, they finally left her, promising another dinner out.

Breaking into her fantasy and memories, her alarm clock rang with the first signal. She buried her face in the pillow and groaned. Time to get up and ready for work. Part of her didn't want to go in, but to find Raphael and Sebastian and spend the day with them instead. The courtship was a time for them to learn about each other.

How could they do that if she was stuck in the office for eight hours a day?

Slapping a hand on the alarm, Hillary grumped while tossing back the covers. She pulled on a robe over the simple chemise she had pulled on after removing the decadent dress and slipped into matching slippers. Pulling the mass of bed hair into a ponytail, she left the bedroom, yawning and stretching.

The coffee machine was already at work, bubbling away on its morning timer, brewing a fresh pot of black coffee. Reaching down for a large mug, she set it next to the brewer and went back to the front door to retrieve the morning papers, one from the city and the other from the clan.

Opening the door, she let out a high-pitched squeak. Pressing a hand to her chest, she jumped back a foot in fright.

"Holy sweet moon! You scared a life out of me," she snapped, staring at her morning visitors.

"*Buenos días, querida.* We're sorry to scare you. We were about to knock right before you opened it," Raphael said, beaming from his spot. He held out the two papers. "Were you coming out for these?"

Trying to swallow her heart back down her throat, Hillary moved a hand against her wild morning hair and plain face. She closed her robe. She couldn't believe they saw her in this messy morning condition. "Ahh, yes, I was. What are you two doing here?"

"We couldn't stay away any longer. We decided to make a delicious breakfast and bring it to you before you went to work," Raphael said, stepping into the house, wrapping his free arm around her waist to pull her aside.

"Good morning, sweet Hillary. I hope you enjoy breakfast in the morning," Sebastian said as he stepped forward, holding a large basket in his hands. He leaned to the side and kissed her cheek. "You look beautiful in the morning, all fresh and dewy."

"I'm a wreck with bed hair and rumpled clothes," she said, shaking her head.

"Nah, it's perfect how you look. Fresh and normal, without all the fuss and primp. I enjoy this version," Sebastian said.

"Thank you, Sebastian. I still can't believe you two are here so early."

"As Raphael said, we can't stay away from our mate. It's our courtship. Where is the kitchen, darling?"

"Ahh, this way. Can I help?" She pointed the way from Raphael's arms and then led them through the small townhouse into the kitchen. She pulled gently away from Raphael when they entered the L-shaped kitchen and morning nook. Moving to the brewer, she reached into the cabinet and pulled down another pair of mugs.

Sebastian set the basket on the counter and pulled out a plate filled high with thick, fragrant French toast slices, another with slices of center-cut bacon, a bowl full of hearty hash brown casserole, and a final bowl of fresh-cut seasonal fruit. He handed the plates and bowls to Raphael, who arranged them on the small kitchen table.

"Plates and silverware, darling, would be wonderful," Sebastian said.

"Did you bring the maple syrup, butter, and powdered sugar?" Raphael asked, peeking into the basket.

"Oh no, did I forget them?"

"Bastian!"

"I'm sorry, Rafe, we were in a hurry. I forgot."

"Don't worry, I have all three," Hillary said before they could argue. She handed Raphael the requested plates, silverware, and added cotton napkins. "Put these on the table. Sebastian, set up the coffee, please. I have sugar and creamer in the fridge, along with the butter tray." She moved to the pantry for the maple syrup and powdered sugar.

"How do you take your coffee?" Sebastian called out.

"Black with two sugars."

"No cream?"

"Not for this kitty," she said, returning to the table after gathering a spoon for the powdered sugar and a knife for the butter. She noticed one of the toms raided her silverware drawer for serving utensils.

Raphael pulled out her chair and helped her settle down before handing her a napkin.

"This is wonderful, much better than the bowl of oatmeal and piece of toast I planned for this morning," she said with a chuckle.

"That is no way to feed a jaguar. How could you stand eating only that until lunch? You must be starving," Sebastian said while they filled their plates with food.

Both toms noticed she took far less than a jaguar should from the scrumptious feast.

"I am a little hungry come lunch, but I'm watching my weight."

"Bah! Ridiculous. Our metabolisms aren't like humans'. You starve yourself, your body will put on more weight, not lose it. You need to eat, Hillary," Raphael said.

"That isn't true. Where did you hear that?"

"It is the truth. Every jaguar knows we need double the calories of a normal human male and female. That's just to maintain our normal body weight and metabolism. If we're highly active or shifting, we need even more."

"That isn't what my father told me," she said in a low tone. "I'm supposed to eat the same as or less than a human female, preferably less."

"Again, it isn't true. We've been in guardian training, and this is the first thing we were told. Now, shall I fill up your plate or let you eat that first and give you another portion?"

She looked at her plate and then the toms. "I'll take another plate after this one." She cut of a thick chunk of the toast and bacon and placed it in her mouth. Her eyes closed at the richness of the toast, the burst of cinnamon and vanilla on her tongue followed by the crispness and crunch of the bacon. "It's delicious."

"Thank you, our recipe," Sebastian said.

Chuckling with Raphael over how Sebastian's chest puffed up with pride in the recipe, Hillary found herself devouring everything on her plate and more. It was a grand feast, which satisfied her purring jaguar.

Afterward, the toms insisted on cleaning the kitchen while she got dressed for work. Feeling so ladylike under their gazes, Hillary pulled on a ruffled, trim skirt in a beautiful print, paired it with a cream silk T-shirt, and topped it off with a cable cardigan she buttoned and accessorized with matching belt, handbag, and heels. A quick fix of her bed hair turned it into an elegant updo with a flounce of curls that settled around her face. She added a light touch of makeup and the same spritz of perfume. A simple watch and earrings pulled the entire look together.

Walking out, she saw the toms finishing putting their dishes back in the basket and wiping clean the table and counters. Everything else they washed and put back in the cabinets or drawers, even the condiments they used. They were lingering at the table with another cup of coffee each and glancing through the two papers.

"Ahh, there you are, looking even more beautiful than before," Raphael said, glancing up from the paper and rising when she entered the room.

"Perhaps I felt a reason to get dressed up this morning. More so than usual," she said, stepping up and accepting his kiss.

"Anything to help motivate a gorgeous lady," Sebastian said, closing the clan's paper and dropping a hand on it. He leaned over and kissed her.

"Do I not want to read the paper this morning, Sebastian?"

"There's an article about us at the restaurant last evening," he said, glancing at Raphael then back to her.

"I figured there would be something since we created quite a disturbance amongst the High Alpha and his party. Is it flattering?"

"Does it have to be?"

She shrugged. "Would make things easier to handle in the office. I know a certain bitch feline who will stomp her way to my floor and make life hell."

"We can join you..."

"No," she said, holding up her hand. "I need to stand as strong as you if this triad is to hold true. I can handle her."

"They made a note about the courtship and our bringing it back to circumvent the dance and laws of the clan," Sebastian said.

"So they're twisting it to make the High Alpha and council come out on top, as they normally have since I've been here. It was the same at home."

"More people will come to realize the good courtship can bring to the clan as they see us fit our lives together before the mating dance," Raphael assured her.

"I hope what you say is true." She glanced at her watch. "I need to get going or I'll be late and I don't think that will make the best of impressions."

"We'll take you," Raphael said.

"You don't—"

"Gives us the reason to take you to lunch and pick you up after work. All the more time we can spend together," Raphael interrupted her.

"I truly wish I didn't have to work at all. I would rather spend the day with you, but being so new to the clan and the job, I don't want to risk it."

"We understand, *querida*. We'll be fine. Besides, we wouldn't expect you to sit at home after the dance."

"Come, let us get going," Sebastian said, herding all of them to the door.

"Such a treat. Breakfast with my toms and a ride to work." Hillary smiled as she took their hands.

"Only the best for you."

Chapter 9

Diving into her work, staying within the confines of her cubicle or Marcus's office to avoid the questioning stares and crowds, Hillary barely noticed how the hours passed. When the accounting program ran smooth for the second time, she pushed back from the double monitors and stretched her arms back over her head.

Strong hands gripped her wrists and helped prolong the stretch in a delicious way that elongated her scrunched spine. She moaned in near delight at the help before turning her head. A warm smile lit up her face.

"Sebastian! What a surprise to see you here," she said, rising and flowing into his arms for a powerful hug.

"Afternoon, sweet kitty," he said, nuzzling his face against her neck. "You didn't even hear me walk behind you."

"How long were you standing here?"

"About ten minutes. I enjoyed watching you work," he said, releasing her to let her sit back down. He crossed his arms over the cubicle wall and rested his head on them.

Looking around for his dark-haired partner, Hillary returned her gaze to him, quirking up an eyebrow. "Where is Raphael? Is he all right?"

"He's fine, Hillary. Something came up at the bar, so he went to take care of things there. Sent his apologies for missing our lunch, but insisted that I not miss it."

"Nothing too bad, I hope?"

"No, typical stuff that just needs one of us present. He'll call if he needs me, but we have others who work with us and know various procedures to give him a hand."

Stroking her fingers along his arm, Hillary nodded in satisfaction and sat in her chair. "I'm sorry he can't make lunch. Perhaps we can bring it to him. Is that practical?"

Sebastian shook his head, but smiled. "Not really. Inventory is coming in, and it'll be a little crazy, but he would have loved the idea."

"Hmm, you'll have to teach me the bar's schedule so I can adjust to it as things move along with the courtship and dance. Perhaps I'll talk to Marcus about shifting my schedule here or something."

"Talk to me about what, Hillary? Hello, Sebastian." Marcus spoke while he walked around the cubicle and leaned against the other wall. He nodded to the superior alpha of the clan and held out a hand.

"Marcus, good to see you again. How have you been?" Sebastian asked, shaking the other male's hand.

"Doing as well as can be expected. Things moving smooth around here. How are Raphael and the bar? Business doing well?"

"Raphael is excellent. We both are now that things are looking up for us," Sebastian said, smiling in Hillary's direction. "The bar is also going well. Every night we're open it's packed. It speaks well for us. Thanks for the program you created. It makes our accounting and inventory work smooth, with far fewer mistakes, especially behind the bar."

"Good to hear." Marcus glanced at Hillary. "How's that new program?"

"Finished, ran the last tests and it's flawless, no bugs to report. You're good for the final testing phase with the accounting group," she said.

"Excellent work, as always," Marcus said. He glanced at Sebastian. "You here to take Hillary to lunch?"

"If you don't mind, yes."

Marcus chuckled and shook his head. "No, I'm pleased about this delightful match for all of you. In fact, Hillary, there isn't another project in the works for you to handle. So…"

"So?" Hillary lifted an eyebrow when her boss trailed off.

"I suggest taking the rest of the week off and spending it with Sebastian and Raphael. The three of you have a lot to discuss and work out before the moon. After the moon dance, things will be heated, minds not quite clear to talk about everyday matters." Marcus grinned and winked at them.

Hillary felt her cheeks flush dark at what Marcus spoke about without mentioning.

Chuckling warmly, Sebastian moved around the cubicle and crouched next to her. He traced his fingers over her arm in a light movement before settling them over her wrist. He raised her arm and kissed her inner wrist. Nuzzling his cheek into her palm, he stared into her eyes.

"It's the heat of the dance, draws out the sexual side of our jaguars to complete the mating. There is nothing to be ashamed about what happens, but a gift of the Fire Moon Goddess who blesses our clan and the mating," Sebastian said. "Raphael and I will take tender care with you during this mating need, introducing you to the wonders of the gifts our Goddess gives us. We were honored to be given her blessing once and we hope our Goddess will bless us again with you."

Leaning over, Hillary nuzzled Sebastian back, remaining quiet.

"Exactly, so please, take this time to get to know one another. Consider it a moon gift from me. Things are quiet in the office. I can handle anything that rises with the accounting program." Marcus dropped a hand on Sebastian's shoulder.

Sebastian glanced up from Hillary. "Thank you for your generous gift, Marcus."

"More than welcome, Sebastian. Go on and take Hillary to a wonderful lunch and far away from here. There's no need to return anytime soon." Marcus winked. "I'll see all of you at the dance."

Standing, Sebastian helped Hillary out of her chair. "Of course we will. Hillary will need you as her sponsor. I hope you'll stand for her."

"It would be my honor," Marcus said with a bow.

"Valerie, will you assist me as well?" Hillary called out to the older kin female.

Rising and leaving her cubicle, Valerie clasped her hands together. "Oh, Hillary, of course I will assist. What an honor." She clasped Hillary in a hug and kissed her cheek. She pulled back and cupped the younger female's cheek. "Thank you for asking."

Hillary hugged Valerie back. "I would ask no one else to stand in place of my mother. Nor could I have a better sponsor than you, Marcus." She stepped from Valerie and hugged Marcus. "Thank you for everything."

"You earned it and more. Enjoy your time until and after the dance. Now go, you two." Marcus laughed while hugging her back and then pushed her back into Sebastian's arms.

Tugging her close, Sebastian kissed Hillary's temple. "Don't have to tell me twice."

Snatching up her purse, Hillary waved to them and let Sebastian lead her out of the office and back into the warm afternoon.

"So, what should we do since we have the whole afternoon?" she asked while sliding into the car.

"First, start with our planned lunch. After that, we'll take it as it happens."

"Sounds like a wonderful plan."

Chapter 10

After a wonderful picnic lunch behind Sebastian and Raphael's house under an ancient oak tree, learning all about their pasts, laughing at their antics, Hillary didn't want to leave. She found herself content and safe in a way she never did back home under her father's watchful eye and roof. Sebastian's gentle care and attention were so different in how he handled her during their time together.

Still, she let him pull her to her feet and escort her home. She linked her arms around his neck to enjoy a tender kiss.

"How you make it hard to leave you," he teased, nuzzling her lips with his. He pulled back, settling hands on her hips.

"Then don't, stay until Raphael gets free and we'll have dinner here."

Sebastian shook his head. "No, we must go out and complete the second night out of courtship. We have reservations at Serenade for dinner."

"Must we?"

With a shrug of his powerful shoulders, Sebastian nodded. "I don't make the laws, darling, I only find them and follow them. Our Goddess will thank us upon the dance. Then we'll be free to do as we please."

"Why must we go out again?"

"Part of the courtship is for others of the clan to see how we get along with one another before the dance. This is how the clan proceeded to find mates before the lighter dances where it was all about sex. Courtship isn't about sex, Hillary. It's about finding a life partner. We talk, laugh, work, and play together to learn about each other. Everyone needs to see we are doing this."

"You're hoping others will follow us and stop the minor dances."

Sebastian nodded. "It would be a wonderful thing. To stop the mindless search by the dance. To live in a world where those who know they wish to be mates can court one another and complete the courtship and mating under the grace of our Goddess."

Hillary leaned over and kissed his lips. "I hope it can be so for the younger kin." She trailed her fingers down his cheek.

"Go inside, I believe Raphael dropped off the new dress and jewels we chose for you."

"Another new outfit?"

"All part of our courtship."

"You're spoiling me."

"Pleasuring you. Enhancing your beauty," he said, kissing her lips.

"What did you get for me?"

"You'll see." He plucked the key from her hand and opened the lock. "Now go inside. Raphael and I will see you in two hours. If you wish to go to the salon, just tell Shayla to put it on our bill."

"You two are too much. No, I can handle my own beauty routine," she said with another kiss. Snatching the key back, she opened the door and slipped inside, listening to his delighted laughter.

Turning away from the door, she saw another trail of soft petals covering the wood floor hallway.

"Raphael, what have you been up to all this time?" she asked the missing tom, shaking her head while breathing in the delicate fragrance of the petals.

Moving down the hallway to her bedroom, she tossed her purse on the bed and kicked off her heels. She went to the closet to remove her work clothes and saw the hanging garment bag on the door. A note pinned to the cover.

Hope you enjoy this dress. I know you'll look ravishing in it, querida.

Sincerely, R

Zipping open the cover, Hillary gasped at the elegant, draped gown hanging from the padded hanger. Created from a fall of watered bronze silk with touches of black lace, the designer draped it in an A-line fashion with one full sleeve, gathered around her waist, before falling to the ground with a thigh-high slit. Black lace edged the sleeve and the full leg slit. Around the hanger, Raphael added a unique necklace created from amber stones and black pearls with matching earrings and bracelet. She found more gifts of silky black lingerie, black spindly heels, a matching clutch, and a gorgeous black comb attached in a clear shoe bag. The comb covered with the same amber stones and black pearls were accents to go in her hair.

After a long soak in the tub, she styled her hair in a beautiful chignon, more elegant than her day look, and fixed it in place with the comb. With another wiggle and fight with the shapewear, she dressed in the new lingerie and gown. As she finished dressing, she heard Raphael and Sebastian knock and enter her home.

Laughing at how they were always early, perhaps to catch her naked, she allowed them to help her with the jewelry, heels, and clutch, as they had the night before. She spritzed the Summertime perfume at her neck and cleavage once more since they enjoyed the scent mingling with her natural feline aroma.

Finished, she linked arms with her toms and let them escort her from home and to the restaurant, Serenade, which a member of the clan had created. She found herself enjoying this restaurant, elegant and regal on the inside, more than the first.

By the time their dinners came, they each helped to feed the other from the different plates, sharing the courses. They teased her, she teased them about their endless appetites, and they got back at her about her finding her own appetite. She whacked both of them on the arm, as they laughed the night away.

However, members of the clan came over to speak with them, eager to talk about the ways and idea of courtship. Most were the younger toms, who wished to speak with a young lady of their choice but couldn't meet up during the dance due to the moon, their families, or the elders. Only now, courtship opened a new pathway for younger cats.

Indulgent to the toms in need, never condescending or arrogant in any fashion, Sebastian and Raphael answered the multitude of questions tossed their way. If a shy female asked a question, Hillary smiled and took her hand to answer. Encouragement and support was the key. It would be their focus to teach the youngsters about the courtship rules—how it wasn't about a sexual relationship, but something else, something deeper. They were focusing on the connection between their hearts and souls instead of the sex.

Other members queried how Hillary felt after the incident with her father, but kept their comments comforting and supportive. There wasn't a hint of gossip-type nature behind the questions, which let her know most of the kin were behind her.

Until the High Alpha stopped by their table on his way out. Again, he looked down his nose at her. "Your father's been informed of your behavior. He wasn't pleased."

"He never is when it comes to me," Hillary said, lifting her chin in temper and pride. "I no longer care about his position."

"He is a High Alpha and important jaguar. As a temporary jaguar in my clan, you should be concerned about your behavior," the older jaguar said.

"Are you accusing our chosen of something? Or threatening her?" Sebastian asked, tossing his napkin on the table.

"Sebastian, no, please," Hillary said, placing a hand on his forearm, feeling his muscles clenched under his jacket and shirt.

"You may have claimed courtship, but she is still a temporary jaguar, not a member," High Alpha Thurston said.

"Regardless of her status, High Alpha, if the Goddess blesses us, she is our mate. We are all full members of this clan. My line is as ancient as yours. Be aware of your position," Sebastian said.

"You threaten me?"

"You dare to threaten my mate," Sebastian said, snarling in anger. "I fought against you when you tried to pull this with Raphael. I will fight again for Hillary."

"Only this time, Sebastian doesn't have to fight alone," Raphael spoke, rising on Hillary's other side.

"The council will hear of this," Thurston said.

"So will the guardians," Sebastian snarled.

Without another word, Thurston moved away, grabbing his wife by her elbow and escorting her out the door.

Glancing around the restaurant as if he appeared to be checking for threats, Sebastian growled low before settling back in his chair. When she stroked a hand on his arm, it calmed him. When Raphael sat next to them, Hillary calmed him as well, stroking his cheek with her fingers.

"Damn him. He needs to be removed from the council," Sebastian growled, shaking out his napkin. He picked up the wine glass and finished the wine in one long sip.

"Calm, my jaguar, calm," Hillary said, tracing his cheek now with her warm fingers. "He is gone. Let's enjoy the rest of our evening."

Beside them, Raphael snarled in Spanish, draining his own glass.

Fearing for her toms, for what the alpha said to her father, Hillary stared at the table as the darkness stayed with them. She nodded to the waiter, who came over with the bottle and refilled their glasses. She watched her toms gulp the wine, feeling the jaguars swirling inside them. She dropped her hands to their thighs, stroking them, and felt Sebastian stretch an arm across the back of her chair in protection. Remaining quiet, she purred softly, giving them her quiet touch and comfort until they settled.

Chapter 11

Things started to return to where they had been before the High Alpha interrupted, but an awkward tension remained between them by the time the waiter dropped the dessert menu on the table. Though everything looked and smelled delicious on their plates, Hillary found her appetite diminished since the High Alpha's talk. Word of her father often did that to her.

Hillary sipped on her wine, fingers restless on the table under Raphael's scrutiny. He often captured and pressed kisses to them.

Before she could lift a fork to continue their meal, her cell phone trilled a familiar tone. A deep church bells tone alerted her to a single caller. Her stomach flipped and plummeted. All attempt at having an appetite disappeared.

The wonderful night was over.

"Damn it," she cursed.

Seconds later, the bells began anew.

Then again.

Then again.

Her eyes closed at the foreboding sound echoing from her purse.

"Turn it off. Let's finish our night," Sebastian said.

"Good idea. Turn it off, *querida*," Raphael said.

Opening her eyes, she studied Sebastian's caring face, then the concerned look upon Raphael's darker face.

"Hillary?" Sebastian asked.

"I can't," she said, her voice breaking.

Raphael tilted his head and stared at her. "*Por favor*, you asked us to continue with the evening. Now, we're requesting the same from you. Just turn off the phone."

"I can't do that."

"Why not?"

"There are multiple reasons that I can't explain to both of you. Believe me when I tell you that I can't ignore the call. Not with this caller, not this time. I'm so sorry."

The toms looked at one another.

Sebastian nodded. "Very well, we'll accept that answer for now."

She cupped a hand to his cheek.

The phone began to ring again.

"Please excuse me. I'll take this call away from the table to not disturb anyone else," she said.

"You don't need to leave us."

"Yes, yes, I do with this conversation." Pressing the napkin to the corners of her mouth, she moved to rise.

Raphael rose to pull her chair out. "Do you want us to follow?"

Sebastian stood on the other side.

Stopping short, she turned, her eyes widened at the thought of them overhearing her pleas and kowtowing to her father. She shook her head with a passionate plea. "No, thank you. It is best I handle this call on my own."

Raphael glanced at his partner, who shook his head and silently agreed. "We'll wait here for you to return to us."

Tossing the napkin aside, she nodded to his words, not hearing them, and rushed away. She pulled the phone out of the purse as it started a third set of rings.

He would not be happy to call her three times. He would be furious with her by now.

Stepping out into the front area, she flipped it open and closed her eyes. "Hello, Father."

"What the hell have you done? Have you lost your mind, girl? I knew I shouldn't have let you out of my sight," Franklin Kearney shouted.

"Father?"

Listening to the latest torrent from him, she saw a black Lincoln pull in front of the restaurant and park. A driver she recognized from home stepped out, went to the back door, and opened it. Her stomach sunk further. Her father was here, in the territory.

"Do you see a Lincoln in front of the restaurant?"

She couldn't lie, he would know. "Yes, sir."

"Get in now."

"I can't leave my companions."

"Get in the car, Hillary, before I do something we both regret."

Looking back to the restaurant, heart cracking, Hillary moved through the doors, into the cool night, and slid into the cavernous backseat.

Chapter 12

"This isn't right!" Raphael growled, shoving the plate of food away from himself. He snatched the napkin off his lap and tossed it on the table. Fingernails tapped out a random pattern on the table.

Glancing around to see the other diners turning to see Raphael's outburst, Sebastian touched his partner's hand. "Raphael, you must calm yourself."

"I can't, not when she's out of our sight. Especially after that look in her eyes. Something scared her."

"I know, but…"

"But nothing. We're all jaguars. Nothing to hide from them." Raphael slashed a hand through the air. "We should never let her go off on her own. We're her mates. She's ours, Sebastian."

Sebastian pushed back the plate of food, appetite forgotten the moment the phone rang. His heart clenched at the sight of fear in Hillary's beautiful eyes. "She didn't want our help. She insisted."

"Regardless. It's our right as toms to be with our female. We serve to protect our female. It is why we're doing this, why we chose her."

"We chose her for more than that reason."

Raphael snarled, snatched up the wine glass, and swallowed the remaining claret liquid. He waved the waiter over to refill his glass. "What good are we doing sitting here? Staring at cooling meat on china?"

Their waiter, Stefan, stepped up with the bottle of wine. "Gentlemen, is there something wrong with your steaks? I can send them back to the kitchen if they're not to your liking. Perhaps I could interest you in something else from the menu," he said while filling Raphael's glass.

"No, there is nothing wrong with our meal, just our appetites. Stefan, please send our apologies to the chef of our injustice to his plates. I'm sure everything was delicious," Sebastian said in a polite tone while Raphael ground his teeth.

"I will pass on your words, sir. What about the lady? Shall I wait before taking your plates away?"

"Yes, give us a few more minutes. She had to take an important call out front."

"Of course, things often come up with this constantly connected world. It happens. Would you like a refill?" Stefan tilted the bottle.

"Please." Sebastian moved his glass over.

Snarling under his breath, Raphael grabbed his glass, swirled the deep red liquid, and swallowed a few gulps.

"Actually, could you do us a favor, Stefan?" Sebastian asked when the waiter finished.

"Of course. What is it?"

"Go out to the front and see how our lady is faring. She seemed upset when the call came in, but didn't want us to see. You know how ladies are," Sebastian said with a grin.

The waiter grinned back and nodded. "Kin females are a mysterious breed. I will check in on her and report back."

"We are only starting to figure out how mysterious. Thank you, Stefan."

Setting the bottle on the table, the young kin male hurried off through the restaurant on his spy errand.

"There. Are you happy now? We have ourselves a spy," Sebastian said to his snarling, grouchy partner.

"No, we should get up, scoop her into our arms, and take her home," Raphael said.

"Hide her away from whatever her troubles are?"

"*Exactamente!*" Raphael pointed a finger at his companion, slamming the glass on the table.

Sebastian chuckled and shook his head. Placing his fingers around the stem of his glass, he busied himself with twisting the glass back and forth, staring at the liquid while waiting for Stefan to return.

"Ah, sweet Goddess, this is *loco*. How long can a phone call last?"

"As long as it must, Rafe."

"What if she needs us?"

"What if she doesn't? She's a strong kitty."

"So vulnerable and innocent to many things though, only putting on that strong exterior front to protect herself. Don't be fooled by that front. She's been hurt. I saw that hurt."

Sebastian looked away from the liquid to his partner. He saw the darkness in those beautiful chocolate eyes. "Someone close?"

"Like someone-on-the-other-side-of-the-phone-call close."

"You're grasping at tails."

"I could be, but we don't know unless we ask."

"That's prying into something she doesn't want to talk about."

"If we're mates, we need to open up."

"Slowly, Rafe, we must go slowly with her. She is young, an innocent."

"Yet we both suggested taking her to Twilight?"

"That is different. Xavier will take the same gentle care with her."

Growling, Raphael leaned back in the chair. He nodded to a direction across from them. "Here comes Stefan."

Sebastian turned his head as Stefan rushed over.

"Is she all right?" Sebastian asked.

"She isn't there," Stefan said.

"What?"

"What in the name of our Goddess did you say?" Raphael rose to his feet, planting hands on the table.

Stefan froze in front of Raphael's anger.

"Stefan, look at me," Sebastian said, rising and taking hold of the young tom's arm. "What did you find out? Where is she?"

"Emile, our maître d', saw her on the phone, and then she went outside and got into a black Lincoln. It drove away. About ten minutes ago," Stefan said. "I'm sorry, sir."

"Damn it! She's gone and could be hurt! We have to find her!" Raphael slammed a fist on the table. He stormed through the tables, heading for the entrance.

"Son of a..." Sebastian shoved a hand through his hair. He snagged his wallet, pulled out a hundred, and shoved it in the waiter's hand. "Meal and tip. Thank you."

"This is too much. You barely ate your meals," Stefan said.

"Not for what you did. Good night." Sebastian rushed after Raphael. He noticed a few other guardian toms rose from their tables to follow.

Outside the entrance, jaguar skills took over so that they could trace Hillary and the Lincoln.

"*Miedo!* She's so scared. She didn't want to get inside, but she did," Raphael said, crouching to scent the air and ground. His eyes glittered with anger.

Sebastian yanked off his tie, watch, and wallet. With a growl, he handed them over to Raphael for keeping.

"What is this?"

"What do you think? I'm shifting now. Follow my tail by car. We're finding her now and going to get the son of a bitch who dared to steal our mate."

"Why you?"

"'Cause now I'm pissed off. This bastard is going down under my claws and no one else's. Not even yours." Sebastian stalked off to the forest to change. He wasn't sure if another jaguar had brought a mortal into the restaurant and didn't know everything about their world. He couldn't chance a mortal seeing the transformation.

They all knew better than to piss off Sebastian Haywood. One of the largest cats of the clan, Sebastian was a fierce hunter but knew when to curb his power and strength. Until someone got on his bad side, then that strength and aggression was unleashed upon that poor soul under his claws and teeth.

"Mount up. We're going hunting," Raphael called out, racing for his car to follow a jaguar and reclaim their mate.

Chapter 13

Hillary didn't remember the trip back to her townhome. She blanked out on how the tom gripped her elbow, dragged her inside, and forced her to sit on the sofa under her father's glare.

"Did you believe I would send you here without keeping checks on you? Hmm? I knew about this 'courtship' thing the moment those damn flowers arrived. Then a damn call from Thurston," Franklin Kearney snapped, towering over her curled up body.

"Couldn't even trust me a little bit? Could you?"

The answer was a backhand across her cheek. The power behind it sent her flailing down the sofa.

Gasping in pain, she covered her cheek with a hand. Staring up at her father's outraged face, she couldn't believe he hit her in such a fashion.

"Little bitch! No better than your mother."

"I didn't do anything wrong!"

"Wrong?" He snatched hold of the gorgeous comb in her hair.

"Father!"

Dragging it from the chignon, he didn't stop until it finally released. With it came a good chunk of hair, causing her to scream. He tossed it in her face.

"What the hell is that?"

Eyes glazed in pain and tears, Hillary contemplated her father's rage with disbelief. "A hair comb. It's a simple hair accessory."

"A simple accessory with amber stones and pearls? What about those damn jewels? That dress?"

She pressed a hand to her necklace, not wanting him to tear it from her neck. "Gifts from Sebastian and Raphael during our courtship. Simple gifts."

"For fucking them. Gifts for a paid whore."

Her jaw dropped, stunned he would call her such a horrible name. "No, I never touched them."

He backhanded her again, catching her on the cheekbone.

Pain radiated out across her face.

"Just what she said." He paced. Long-legged strides ate up the tiny space she kept so tidy. He crumpled and stomped over the delicate petals carefully strewn for a second night by Raphael, who knew how much she loved it the first time. Now those soft petals were ground to nothing under the shiny heels of her father's hundred-dollar loafers from London.

"Why did you send me then?"

"Perhaps, I thought you would grow up a little bit. Ha! What a laugh. Look at the mess you created, little bitch of mine."

"What mess are you referring to? With the blessing of the Fire Moon Goddess, I will be the treasured mate of two powerful toms and guardians of this clan. They are respected kin members. One of them from an ancient line of the Fire Moon Clan. It's what you wanted for me."

He stopped and stared. He dropped down, scooped up some ground up petals, and tossed them in her face. "This? You think these mean anything to me. To them?"

She winced as they floated over her. "They mean something to me! They care for me! It's why they chosen the path of courtship, to prove their love before the dance. They've done nothing to hurt me."

"They will use you and drop you! What use will you be to me then? Nothing!"

"It's not like that, Father! They are my mates! Please! They chose courtship over a mating dance to prove it's not only sexual between us."

"Mates? Mates? They are gay, daughter! They fuck each other. Not stupid little girls like you. They are using you."

"You're wrong!"

He slapped her. "Never talk to me in such a fashion! You know better!"

She cringed under the harsh attack and flurry of slaps and hits.

"They played this game before. Now they're playing it on you. Wake up and smell the bullshit."

"No, not them. Not this time. This is different. They promised me!"

He laughed in a braying, harsh tone. His hand came down on her cheek again. "Different? Different? Promise? Words, just words. Stupid little girl!" He slapped her, hitting her after every question.

She screamed in pain.

"How dare you accept a courtship from two mated gay toms? Unacceptable. This will not happen! Do you hear me, daughter? This is against all of my orders and plans for you. I will not have this happen. This is highly unacceptable," Franklin shouted, reaching out and grabbing hold of her hair.

"They are my mates, Father. We have the dreams, the energy, everything," she screamed in pain, reaching up to hold his wrist and her hair.

"Dreams and energy can be faked! You are here for one purpose only, little bitch. You are here because of me! For my purpose! Mine!"

"Father, please! You're hurting me!" Tears ran down her face.

"Do you hear me? I don't care if you fucked them. You will not dance with them! There will be no dance for you."

"What? No, Father, no. They're my mates."

Tossing her aside, he slapped her again, then again.

Lying on the area rug, she huddled, cheeks reddened from his hand, crying in pain and fear. "Father, please."

"You will not marry some damn homosexual toms. Do you hear me? You are here for one purpose, to mate with a member of the High Alpha family."

"I can't, Father," she whimpered.

"Why would say that to me?" He leaned over her, ready to kick her.

"Joshua took Belinda Alcott as mate."

"You thought I meant that little bastard? He is nothing. I never bargained for him. He was only a testing ground to see if the High Alpha meant his word to me during the signing papers for your transfer."

"What word? What have you done to bring me here?"

"The High Alpha is recalling his middle son from another clan. He will be here before the moon. This son will be the new High Alpha, not the first son, who is weak, addicted to drugs by a corrupt mate. You will dance and mate with him this Friday. Through you, I will have control over two powerful clans," Franklin said, a satisfied smirk on his face.

"Like hell she will."

Chapter 14

A jaguar's ferocious growl and scream broke through the silence, waking everyone in the neighborhood, possibly within the territory. It would alert all guardians what was happening within the townhome and send them running.

Standing near the powerful golden cat, one hand resting on its shoulders, Raphael wanted to transform as well when he surveyed the horrendous scene. Their beloved female huddled upon the area rug and hardwood floor, surrounded by ground up petals, a tall tom leaning over, ready to strike another fearsome blow. Another male stood to the side, arms crossed over his chest, doing nothing to protect the female.

Underneath his hand, he felt the muscles bunch and coil with power, ready to strike against the males who had unleashed harm on a female. Not just any female of the kin, but their chosen mate.

Sebastian snarled and dropped into a lowered crouch on his large paws. Lethal talons appeared from his paws, dug into the wood floor, and gave him the killing edge to pounce on the attacker of their chosen.

"Contain and damage to your heart's content, but do not kill, Sebastian. Justice must be met for this one," Raphael ordered.

Sebastian snarled in displeasure at the order.

"Do not *matar*," Raphael repeated.

Franklin Kearney let out a high-pitched scream when the huge jaguar leaped and landed on him. He raised arms and legs to block the claws and jaws.

It was pointless.

Doing considerable damage to the man, Sebastian gripped the horrid man's neck in his powerful jaws and held still. He wanted to snap the bones, but didn't.

Justice for Hillary would not come from a swift death. A trial with proof of his actions against her was what she needed. The Elders needed to know what this alpha did to his own daughter and the two clans.

He held back the final blow as ordered, waiting for the guardians.

* * * *

Knowing his partner would do what was necessary, Raphael rushed to the crumpled form of their mate. He hollered in pain and anger at the sight of her curled in fetal position, cheeks reddened from slaps and hits, tears streamed down her face, ruined the careful makeup she adored, the beautiful hairdo she loved now in tatters.

On the floor, she curled up tighter at his jaguar's cry of rage. A whimper left her, her arms tightened around her head, protecting her. Tangled black locks strewn over her face.

Feeling his jaguar rise, once again wanting to shift and join Sebastian, Raphael shook himself back. They must care for her. Hillary needed them now, more than ever.

"Hillary, *querida*, ssh, it's Raphael. Sebastian and I are here. We're both here for you. We're here, *mi dulce*. It's over. It's over," he comforted, crouching down to touch her, feeling for any breaks. His fingers touched a few of those silky curls and tugged them back from her swollen face.

At first, she cried out in fear and pain.

"No, *querida*, it's Raphael," he said, turning her to cradle against his chest.

Opening her eyes, she called out in recognition. Shooting up from her curled position like a coiled snake, arms winding hard around his neck, she burrowed her face against his shoulder. Cries became more earnest. Her body trembled in pain and fear.

"Raphael, Raphael, Raphael," she murmured, running his name together.

"I'm here, *gato dulce*, I'm right here. Oh, *dulce* Hillary," he whispered, drawing a hand over her hair and back.

"Sebastian?"

"Handling your father," he answered.

She whimpered in fear.

"It's okay, *querida*. He came to fight in jaguar form. He is more than capable of dealing with the bastard. Have no fear for our Bastian, he's one of the finest toms and guardians of the clan," he reassured.

"He won't be harmed?"

"No, *gato dulce*, he'll be doing the harming, trust me on that."

A rumbled purr escaped as she cuddled against him.

"Let's get you out of here for the meanwhile. Sebastian will join us when the guardians are done with him. He'll be by your side in a few moments."

Nodding, she turned against his chest and fell quiet.

Rising, cradling his beloved package, he went to the bedroom. He needed to take her away from where the guardians would make a careful inspection of what happened between father and daughter. Sebastian would shift and handle their interrogation before joining them. Then they would take Hillary home to recuperate with them. No longer would she sleep alone.

Pausing, he saw a lower guardian and nodded, getting his attention. "Go fetch an ice bag, gel pack, or bag of frozen peas, along with a soft cloth. *Por favor*," he whispered.

The young male nodded and growled at the bound cats. "Damn bastard. How could a father hit his own daughter?"

Raphael shook his head and moved to the bedroom. He rubbed his cheek against her head and settled on her bed. Sliding back until he could pull his legs up, keeping her cradled, he rocked them, comforting both of them, letting her cry.

Long moments passed. Raphael didn't acknowledge the younger male who brought in a cool gel pack and cloth to place on Hillary's face. When she did move her head, he gently maneuvered the pack and cloth until she hissed when the cold pack met her skin.

"Ssh, I know, *mi querida.* Let it do its job. It will take away the sting and swelling." He pressed light kisses along her forehead and temples.

"I'm sorry I left you and Sebastian at the restaurant," she murmured against his chest. She brought her hand up and played with a button on his shirt.

"Was he waiting for you outside?"

"No, sent a car for me. He would never lower himself to personally come and get me. He barked orders to get in over the phone and I obeyed. I always obeyed him."

"You're a dutiful daughter who loves her *padre.* Why shouldn't you do what he asked?"

"Even when he shouts at me?"

"Fathers get angry when children don't always follow his commands."

"Until this evening out with you and Sebastian, I always followed his orders."

Raphael drew back and turned her chin to look at him. "Always?"

She nodded. "That was my role."

Drawing his fingers through her tangled hair, Raphael nodded, massaging her throbbing temple with a thumb. "This what the High Alpha meant?"

She bobbed her head once.

"Oh, Hillary." He leaned his cheek back on her head when she tucked it against his shoulder.

"I thought he would be different after my move. Only, he got worse because I went with my heart."

"You chose us, not him."

Her fingers gripped his shirt, dirty from her tears and mascara.

"Ssh. It's all right. You're safe with us."

The ticking of claws alerted them to another presence before a warm, heavy head dropped on their joint laps. A loud purring noise rose to comfort her.

"Bastian, what are you doing?" Raphael teased, his tone light, when he recognized what his lover tried to do, still in his jaguar form.

The jaguar plopped his bottom down, his tail flicking against the carpet. Large golden eyes, tinted with Sebastian's deep green, peered up at them from the feline face filled with long whiskers, black rosette patterns against the golden fur. Rounded ears turned and moved with the smallest of sounds, but remained focused on them. He lifted a front paw and placed it on the bed near Raphael's knee.

"Sebastian, you're safe," Hillary said, dropping the cold pack, leaning away from Raphael's hold toward the jungle cat. Reaching out with her hands, she hugged the powerful neck, dropping her cheek on its forehead, and rubbed.

The purring increased in volume.

Her nails found the sensitive spots behind Sebastian's ears and scratched, giving him pleasure in return.

Raphael chuckled at their play and caring.

Sebastian nuzzled her in return, marking her with his scent when she moved forward, until Raphael pressed a hand to his chest.

"Oh no, you big idiot, you're not getting on this bed in that form. Go on, get out of here and change. *¡Vamos!*"

The jungle cat growled, issuing a challenge.

Hillary tucked herself against Raphael's side and giggled at their interaction.

"Don't even think about it. It's time to take care of Hillary, not you. *¡Vamos!*" Raphael ordered, pointing a finger.

Shaking his big head, Sebastian turned, flicked his tail off at his lover, and stalked out of the bedroom.

Pressing herself against Raphael's chest, Hillary found herself laughing at the cat's actions under such circumstances. "You got flicked off by a tail."

"I know, how horrible and rude of him. Tell me why I love him again?" Raphael asked in a confused tone.

"He's hot?"

"There's that."

"Good in bed?"

"*Sí...*"

"Loves you back."

Raphael chuckled. "That's a given. I guess I'll put up with him." He hugged her close once more. He lifted the cloth and pack of peas and placed it on the nightstand. "You're gonna have to deal with him, too, you know?"

"That big, mangy pile of fur?"

"*Sí*, he'll be all yours, too."

"Oh, lovely, I'm sure we'll manage him somehow," she said, nuzzling her forehead against his neck for a minute. "What will be done?"

"Something will be said to the Elders about our alpha and your father and this supposed deal they made. That kind of deal should be illegal among all the clans," Sebastian answered, walking into the room. He now wore jogging pants, donated by one of the guardians since he destroyed his suit during the shift to rescue her. He strode to the bed and crouched in front of the bed in his human form.

Hearing Sebastian's voice, Hillary turned away from Raphael's shoulder. When she met his gaze this time, his hands reached to curl around her jaw. "Your jaguar is beautiful."

He smiled at her and then let his smile drop in concern. "Oh, sweetheart." Sebastian noticed Raphael shifted his position to let him get a look at the damage her father had ravaged. "Let me see." His fingers gentle as he pushed back damp curls. He went over some areas, saw her winces and gasps of pain.

"Does it look as bad as it feels?"

Lifting up, he pressed butterfly-light kisses to those swollen areas, then on each closed eyelid. He pulled back, saw her blink and smiled. Running a light finger down her nose, he gave her a proud smile.

"What is that smile for?"

"You're such a strong lady. Do you know how strong you truly are?"

"Me? No. I'm just holding things together, barely keeping my head above water at times. You two are so much stronger than me, emotionally and physically."

Sebastian shook his head. "No, deep inside you're strong. Otherwise, I don't think you would've come through this as well as you did."

Raphael ran his knuckles up and down Hillary's arm, keeping her with them, adding comfort and touch.

"As for this," Sebastian said, moving his finger to her cheek, "Nothing is broken, thank goodness. Let's keep this pack on your cheekbone. It will keep the swelling down. Son of a bitch shouldn't be walking out of here." He reached for the pack, squished the gel to keep it cool, and wrapped it up.

Hillary shook her head. "Don't, please, just let it go."

"He threw you to the ground and hit you hard. Bastard kicked you, baby, and heavens know what else he did before we got to you."

"I know what he did and more, Bastian. It isn't the first time he's done this." She leaned forward and pressed her forehead to his.

"He'll be facing justice," Raphael said.

"After what we saw, we're not letting him walk away without facing justice. Do not ask us to let him leave," Sebastian said.

Letting out a long breath, she nodded. "I understand. I wouldn't ask that from either of you. I understood the limits of kin males from a young age."

"Then give us this at least?"

"I will. Do what you wish with him and your alpha. Make it right."

Raphael leaned up and kissed her forehead.

"Thank you, kitty." Sebastian smiled.

"How long will they be out there?"

"Until things are cleaned for you. They won't leave the mess for you to clean," Raphael said.

Hillary sighed.

"What is it, kitty?"

Somehow, Hillary managed to reach down, grab Sebastian's hand, and raise it to her reddened, swollen face, stained by tears and makeup. She did the same with Raphael.

"Hillary?" Sebastian asked.

"Take me home," she whispered.

"Are you certain of this decision?" Raphael said.

Sebastian added, "We can end things, if you wish."

"Never more certain. No, I don't want us to end." She stared at them in turn. "Take me home. I want our courtship to continue. You were right at the restaurant, no one but us has any right to say what goes on in our bedroom."

They smiled and nodded.

"Take me home."

"Isn't this home?" Raphael asked.

"No, this is temporary housing of my father's choosing. I thought it could be home, but he breached it. No, home is with you, where you are." She shook her head. "Take me home."

"Whatever you wish, darling," Sebastian said.

She gave him a faint smile.

Sebastian placed the pack on her cheek with a gentle kiss on her forehead. "I'll go make the arrangements. Stay here with Raphael."

Chapter 15

After a packing job to get the necessities for Hillary, Sebastian carried her into their house when the guardians let them leave. He demanded it this time since he claimed Raphael already had his chance to hold her tight.

"I can walk," she offered.

"Absolutely not," Sebastian said, before swinging her up in his powerful hold.

Leading her through the home they made theirs, giving her a short tour, Raphael opened the double doors to their bedroom. "That is if you wish to sleep with us. Otherwise, I can show you the guest room. It's right across the hall with your own bathroom." He moved across the hall to the door.

"No, I want your room," she said from Sebastian's arms. "I still wish to hold the rules in place, but I want…I want to be held, cuddled. I don't want to sleep alone."

Her males smiled and Raphael moved back to her. He curled a hand around her cheek.

"Oh, *querida*, we wish to cuddle you all night long. Though it will be such a strain on our umm…" He glanced down with a cockeyed look at the tented erection that got a smile to poke through her pain. "…we will uphold your wishes."

"Exactly, you'll have to excuse the demands of our bodies. They have their own wishes and urges, but we'll keep them under control and all that kind of stuff," Sebastian said with a grin. "As best as possible." His sweats strained across the front as his body reacted to her scent and closeness.

"This always happens to you two?"

They glanced at each other then back to her.

"When you are near us, *sí*," Raphael said, opening the doors to let Sebastian swing her through to settle her on the bed.

"Now we have you in our house, seeing you in our bed, that would be an even bigger yes. It's adding an even bigger claim to you. Our cats want to put their mark on you, on their female," Sebastian explained, brushing past Raphael as he entered the room. Leaning down, he placed her on the bed.

"Oh," she said, blushing. "Will all of this be a problem? Sleeping together?"

"No, no. As promised we will do our best to uphold your wishes to keep to the laws until your desires change to know more," Raphael said.

"As true gentle cats, I knew you would. Though," she said, blushed hard, and pressed against Sebastian's shoulder.

"Hmm, I think our lady wishes to see something naughty and dirty," Raphael teased.

"Oh yes, what would our little one like to see her toms do with each other?" Sebastian joined in on the teasing. He stood next to Raphael, setting up in the same position.

Momentarily glimpsing her males, noticing their mirror positions, Hillary grabbed a pillow and hid behind it. She heard them break up into hilarious laughter at her antics. When she dropped the pillow a little, it was to find them crouched in front of her.

"What is it you wish to see, *mi inocente dulce*?" Raphael asked.

"Loving each other," she whispered.

"With you watching?" Sebastian asked.

She nodded. "I want to know what it's like between you. Before me."

The toms looked at each other. Sebastian ran a hand over the back of his neck. Raphael scratched at his bristled chin.

Groaning at her request, she covered her face with the pillow. "Never mind I asked. Forget the whole idea."

"No, no, we promise to give every request some merit and you wish to see us. Though, you need to know the truth."

"Truth? About what?"

"Two toms are stronger, brutal almost in lovemaking. It's not soft and gentle, Hillary. You will give us that," Raphael said, tugging on the pillow.

"Do you understand that it may not be what you imagine?" Sebastian added.

She dropped the pillow enough for their gazes to meet. She shifted her gaze to look over at Sebastian. "Understand. You're both strong, powerful toms prone to violence and anger, as jaguars can be in the jungle."

"Darling, did anyone make love with you?" Sebastian asked.

She shook her head.

"Any kind of sex?" Raphael asked.

Another simple shake of her head was their answer.

"A lot of teaching before the moon, Raphael," Sebastian said with a wicked grin.

"Oh *sí*, including a whole lot of delectable, sensual, erotic teaching before the moon, Sebastian. Most of it done without breaking the laws. I believe we will be keeping this one home from work to do all this training," Raphael answered with the same grin.

By now, the pillow dropped back to her lap, she was outright staring at them. "Teaching? Teaching me what? How can you without breaking laws? Keeping me home?"

"And there will be lots of toys to introduce and ready your body to accept us," Raphael said. "How else will we get enough time by Friday?"

"What about my work?"

"It can be done here. The entire area is connected and your boss understands. We'll have you hooked up in the morning. Though, our training will come first and you'll enjoy it far more than boring work," Raphael said.

"Don't let her trick you about work," Sebastian said, raising an eyebrow.

Hillary flushed under his stern look.

"What? What am I missing?" Raphael glanced between them.

"Marcus gave me the rest of the week off until the moon and after the dance. There is no...um...work to distract me. You have me all to yourselves," she said.

"This true, *mi amante*?"

"I heard it myself, Rafe. She's all ours."

"And she's sitting right here." Hillary harrumphed, crossing arms under her breasts. "Back to this teaching you two are talking about. This includes toys and you."

"Not just him, but both of us. Working together to bring your body to such delightful heights of pleasure," Sebastian said.

She blinked.

"Perhaps you will take both of us at once, if you say yes. Only when you say *si*. We'll do nothing without your consent. There will be a safe word. Whenever you say it, we *lo terminaremos*. No questions asked. Completely stop and pull away until you are ready," Raphael said.

"Honest truth," Sebastian said.

Hillary looked between them. "Is it always done that way?"

Both toms nodded.

Sebastian added. "It's used if there is more than one partner, or if one is new to something, yes. Especially if a partner cares about another."

"What is a safe word?"

"Something not normally used during that time," Raphael explained.

"Pick one, anything you wish," Sebastian said.

"Vendela," she said.

Raphael raised an eyebrow. "*¿Qué dijo?*"

"The rose you chose for me to announce our courtship."

The toms grinned.

"Vendela it is," Raphael said.

"That was easier than I thought," Sebastian said, nodding in agreement.

Raphael clapped his hands once, rubbed them in a circle. "Next order of business for your decision."

She raised her hands, palms up, and curled her fingers toward herself. She gave them a wicked little grin. "Bring it on."

"Ooh, love that sassy little grin," Sebastian said with a growly meow.

"Calm down, *querida*. Time to care for her, not sex her up. Remember?" Raphael waved him back.

"Yes, no sexing up, just take tender, loving care." Sebastian gave a firm nod of his head.

"Is that the plan of the evening?" Hillary asked.

"After all you went through, hell, yes," Sebastian said.

Her jaw dropped a little at Sebastian's aggressive insistence.

"Would you like a shower, bath, nap, or something else? You went through a wicked last few hours. We wish to wash and comfort it all away."

"Though I would enjoy finding out what the something else is, I don't have the energy. I would also love a long soak, but I really need to sleep. I am so tired," she said.

Grinning, Raphael shrugged, shoving hands in his pockets. "I had a feeling that would be the answer. I can hear the exhaustion in your voice."

Sebastian nodded.

"I wish it could be something else and you're working on helping me head toward the something else, but it's still too soon. I'm in a little pain, but healing. We heal fast. The ice helped and your closeness helped more."

"You do look better. Less flush and swollen," Sebastian said.

"Hmm, thank you, I want to stay up longer and do something else, but—" She stopped as a long yawn escaped.

Raphael held up his hands and shook his head. "Go on to the bathroom and change to your night clothes. Perhaps, a little request though."

"Hmm?"

"Could we help with your other night routines?"

"Like?"

"Your face and hair?" Raphael drew a finger down her cheek.

"I must look like a mess." She covered her face with a hand.

"Ssh…don't even think of apologizing for what happened to us. You have nothing to apologize for because none of it was your fault or doing," Sebastian interrupted before Raphael could, stepping closer, rubbing a knuckle against her hand.

"Exactly, listen to Sebastian, *querida*. You had a rough evening. We wish to make it better." Tilting closer, Raphael pressed a kiss against her temple.

"Give me a few minutes to change then?"

Her toms nodded and left the room.

Chapter 16

Stepping out of the bathroom, dressed in a long nubby cotton robe that hid more than it revealed, Hillary tucked the body shaper deep in the suitcase to hide it from the males. She looked for a hanger and turned to see Sebastian entering with the padded hanger from her home in his hand. She smiled when he took the dress from her and placed it on the hanger.

"Thank you, Sebastian. I was wondering where to put that," she said.

"We need to figure out closet space while settling your things in our home. Not to worry about it tonight, we'll figure everything out in the morning," Sebastian said, turning to open another door, revealing a deep walk-in closet. He hung the hanger from a bar and closed the door. "There's a hamper in the bathroom. You can place the lingerie in there."

Nodding, Hillary turned and saw the wicker basket, and placed the silky things inside. She stepped back out to see Raphael inside the room. He smiled at her while he untucked his shirt. He undid the buttons and then began on the cuff links. Before she could move to help him, he motioned for her to settle back on the bed.

"Come here, Hillary, come and cuddle against me. We're going to let Raphael do most of the work tonight," Sebastian said, tugging her closer by grabbing the edges of the cotton robe. Reaching out, he snatched one of the ties and wrapped it twice around his hand. He used it to bring her against the bed. He then sat on the bed, slid against the headboard to make a nest of the pillows and his body for her. He snuggled her between his legs.

Lifting her bottom up, she twitched the bathrobe around her body. She closed the edges and tugged the tie from his hand. "You're going to behave yourself?"

He grinned, playing a friendly tug-of-war over the tie. "I promise."

Chuckling softly, Hillary shook her head. "Then let go of my tie."

"You gonna stay in place?"

"Yes."

He smiled and released his grip on the tie. Leaning over, he rubbed his bristled cheek against her soft one. He pressed a warm kiss against her ear and neck.

Chuckling at the ticklish sensation of his breath on her ear, she brought up her shoulder and rubbed him and her ear. "Tickles," she teased. Still, she turned and nuzzled him back, exchanging scents with him, letting out a soft purr. She relaxed against the warm tom, letting the tension seep out of her limbs. A long sigh slipped out of her.

Meanwhile, Raphael went to Hillary's bag and poked around until he found the toiletries bag, then the makeup bag.

"There are all types of curious items in here," Raphael said, lifting up an eyebrow.

"Ooh, what are you finding?" Sebastian asked with curiosity in his voice.

"I'm too tired to explain everything tonight to you," she said.

"Perhaps another night. For now, I'll just pull out what I need," Raphael said.

"Hmm, silly toms."

Nodding in pleasure, Raphael found the one he wanted, pulled a cleansing cloth from it, resealed the bottle, and returned to the bed. He settled against Sebastian's leg, not bothering to remove his shirt, and took Hillary's chin between his fingers.

"Now we can see the mysterious procedures females do at night to get ready for bed, Rafe. Perhaps we should give hints to all the other bachelors as warnings to prepare them," Sebastian said, chuckling.

Hillary sent a playful elbow into his belly. "Don't you dare, Bastian, that would take all the fun out of our feminine rights in using the bathroom."

"Ooof, sharp elbow," the tom said, rubbing his abused stomach.

Raphael chuckled and shook his head. "Nah, we'll keep the knowledge to ourselves. I, for one, am pleased to know what happens. After waiting for so long."

She studied him. "Has it been so long for you two?"

"Lifetimes," he whispered.

"Many lifetimes," Sebastian whispered.

"Now, let me cleanse your face, *mi querida dulce*. Then we'll let you get some rest. What side do I use?"

"Doesn't really matter. Both work the same." She closed her eyes so he could remove the remainder of her mascara and eyeliner with the cloth.

After he scrubbed her face clean of makeup and tear tracks with the cloth, he balled it up and tossed it in the trash. He moistened a soft washcloth, drew it across her face with the same care, and then dried her face. He saw a bottle of moisturizer and held it up in question.

"Quarter-size dollop on fingers and smooth all over and on neck."

Nodding, smiling at the directions to take care of their lady, Raphael squeezed out the amount, rubbed his fingers together. After warming the liquid, he smoothed and massaged it into ravaged skin, careful of the cheekbone and some swollen areas.

"Starting to feel better?"

"Hmm, it does help. Thank you, Raphael," she whispered.

"You do this every night?"

She nodded against Sebastian's shoulder.

"Her hair is still tangled from his abuse," Sebastian reminded in a gruff tone.

"Oh, *sí*, we can't leave it all tangled. It will only get worse while you sleep. *Querida*, what do we do with that?" Raphael capped the bottle, returned it, and held up the one with her hair supplies.

She licked her lips. "Wide-tooth comb. Just a comb through at night. I usually sleep in a braid or ponytail."

"We know how to do braids. Let's get rid of those tangles," he said, returning with the comb.

Leaning forward in Sebastian's gentle hold, Hillary sighed as the two males took turns to drag the comb with care through the tangles and snarls. They took longer than she probably did, but she felt sincere pleasure throughout by the time her hair was shiny and smooth. It had the slight curl at the end it got when she combed it right. When finished, Raphael returned the comb to her bag, keeping her things neat and in place as she did at home.

Then Sebastian's larger hands took over, running his fingers through her hair, separating it into larger sections before braiding it with ease. He didn't tug or pull at any time. It sent a soft purr in her throat as she began to drift off into slumber. Taking a holder from Raphael, he secured the ends below her nape, placing a kiss between her shoulder blades.

* * * *

"She's asleep, Bastian." Raphael turned back to see Hillary's eyes closed, her breathing evened out.

"What?"

"She started purring, and then fell asleep while you braided her hair. She trusted us completely enough to let down her guard." He strode closer, steps silent, and sat softly, trying not to jostle their sleeping female.

Sebastian angled his neck to look down at the sleeping cat in his arms and smiled. Neither of them had held a female like this in their arms before, never one so open and trusting that she would fall asleep without a word or warning. He brought up a hand and drew a wayward curl from her flushed face.

"I still want to go and kill her father."

"Same here, *amante*, but justice must be done for her. She deserves that."

Sebastian nodded. "How much longer till the moon?"

"Another three days."

"How will we last?"

"I don't know, but we must. Why do you ask?"

"Part of courtship requires no penetration until confirmation by the fire moon."

Raphael's jaw dropped. He raised a hand and scratched his bristled jaw. "That changes the rules. How far of penetration and for whom?"

"We can't penetrate her with our cocks, Raphael, take her virginity if she is one or if it's our first time with her. Either way, we keep our cocks to ourselves." Sebastian glanced down at his hard and ready member and then his lover's equally erect penis.

"Why didn't you say anything before?"

"Situation never came up?"

"Nice try, *amante*," Raphael said, glowering at his lover. "How will we teach her all the sensual ways of lovemaking without the penetration?"

"We have our ways and knowledge and toys, as we told her. Plus there is everything Xavier taught us at Twilight. All of it, we will put to use now. Take it one step at a time with her, like you said. We must go tender and slowly with our lady."

"Then on the night of the Fire Moon?"

"With the blessing of our Goddess, all restraints are removed from lovemaking. The courtship law allows partners to learn about each other without the feverish need for sex getting in the way like the dances do now. That's why so many mates are unhappy. They don't know each other except in the sexual nature. They don't know their likes or dislikes, wants or needs, nothing beyond the pattern of sex because it's all the dance gave them."

"Or that's all they took from the time of the dance," Raphael pointed out, gently trailing his fingers down Hillary's soft arm. He heard her murmur and snuggle closer against Sebastian's chest, deep in sleep.

"Perhaps the courtship law should be resurrected and the mating dance be removed if we prove how well this works with Hillary at the Fire Moon Dance this weekend."

"That would be a wonderful thing for the young toms and females to have an opportunity to learn and explore one another. Things will already be shaken up with the news of her father and our High Alpha's involvement with her transfer."

"I damn well hope the Council will not demand her return to her previous home."

"Hell no!" Raphael growled.

A warning moan rose from Hillary as she twisted against Sebastian.

The toms fell quiet, waiting for her to fall quiet, her breathing to become even once more.

"Ssh, you'll wake her," Sebastian said.

"*Sí, lo sé, lo sé.*"

"What should we do now?"

Rising, Raphael finished removing his stubborn cufflinks and then the wrinkled dress shirt. Down to his pants, he turned to his lover and their chosen female. With a smile, he gave Sebastian the quintessential pantomime of the "I don't know" shrug.

His lover tried to hold back a chuckle from erupting and disturbing their lady while they contemplated this unknown situation.

"Looks like it's time to sleep," Raphael said, glancing down at their lady. "With her in our arms."

"I can't wait."

Chapter 17

Snuggled in a circle of living warmth, she didn't want to awake from this wonderful dream and back to reality. It pushed back the darkness of the nightmares that tried to invade her sleep. There was nothing more she wanted than to remain here within this cocoon of comfort and safety. A heady combination of masculine scents from her males, soft cotton, cloud-filled pillows, and the tangle of their feet. Then there were their whisperings over her head when they thought she still slept.

"Should we get up? I don't want to disturb her sleep," Sebastian said.

"Same here, she needs her sleep. So beautiful when she sleeps, too," Raphael said. "I heard the coffee machine start. Could use a cup."

"Hmm, same here. Grab me a cup."

"Me? Why me?"

"You're closer to the door."

"If I move, I'll wake her."

"Well, it's the same if I move."

"*Mi diosa dulce*, we never had this issue before," Raphael growled. "I could care less about waking up your lazy butt in the mornings."

"Oh, well thank you very much, Raphael, not that it's a bad issue to have."

"No, definitely not a bad issue, other than this itchy bathrobe of hers. That is something we'll have to remedy. This thing is hideous on her."

"An excuse to go shopping again?"

"Excellent idea, *mi amante*, something short and silky. We can indulge ourselves in the lingerie section."

"Is the lingerie section for her or for us?"

"Complicated question. I'm still figuring that out since the last time we went there for the dress. Though, I thoroughly enjoyed the experience," Raphael said with a warm chuckle.

"I still want coffee," Sebastian said.

"Then get up and get it, *gato holgazán.*"

"I am not a lazy cat!"

"*Sí*, you are!"

"No, it means waking her up and being the bad guy."

"And we're back to the original problem."

Sebastian grumbled something incomprehensible under his breath.

Unable to stop herself, laughter bubbled up to the surface and escaped. She wiggled back and forth in their arms.

"What is this? Sleeping kitty is awake?" Sebastian asked.

"Enough, enough. Yes, I'm awake. I'm awake. You can stop worrying about waking me. I can solve the issue because I want coffee, too, please, so whoever is getting some can get me a cup as well," she said, chuckling, bumping fists in their stomachs.

"You little faker! How long have you been awake?" Sebastian stared down at her. He brushed back some tangles of her hair, nuzzling her cheek with his nose. He burrowed deeper in her hair, breathing in her warm scent, while kissing her earlobe and neckline.

"Only for a few minutes to overhear your dilemma of getting coffee," she said, still chuckling.

Raphael gave a grumbled sigh while he pressed closer to her. "Keeping desperate toms from their coffee while they try not to disturb a sleeping lady only she's faking it, now that's just plain mean. I say…a round of…" He grinned.

"No, Raphael…" Hillary warned, holding up a hand, pressed it against his bare chest.

"Are you saying we should break out those?" Sebastian asked.

"Oh *sí, mi gatito*."

Hillary swung her gaze between them. "You two wouldn't dare."

"Tickle!" they shouted together.

She squealed as the males wiggled their fingers and pounced on her. Laughter rolled from all three of them while they their fingers danced across her body, finding those ticklish places. Between her wiggling and writhing to get away from them and their fingers, her bathrobe loosened and opened.

Soon, she felt calloused fingers graze the warm skin. Another set of fingers found the curve of her breast. Laughter turned into a moan.

"Hillary?" Sebastian asked when her hand gripped his shoulder.

"What happened?" Raphael stared down at them and saw how her robe opened.

Opening her eyes, staring up at them, she pulled in a deep breath and held it. Her breasts full and plump, nipples taut under their gazes. Exhausted after last night, she didn't bother to pull on a nightie, just the robe before slipping into the bed and their arms. Now, she lay bare to their gaze, naked under a masculine gaze for the first time.

Her heart beat faster as their gazes moved languidly from her throat, skimmed her breasts, her rounded belly, the thatch of curls covering her womanhood between her full thighs as she brushed them together. A soft flush covered her upper chest and began a slow climb up her neck as they continued to study her body and all its flaws.

"Sebastian, Raphael, please," she whispered, tugging at the edges of the robe.

"No, *mi dulce*, don't cover up from our gaze," Raphael said.

"Please, let us look upon your femininity and grace." Sebastian lifted a hand and drew a single finger from her neck, between her breasts, and over her belly. He stopped and circled around her belly button.

Her muscles quivered as her breathing shifted and halted.

"Breathe, Hillary," Raphael teased in her ear.

"Don't forget to breathe, beloved," Sebastian whispered.

Air rushed into her lungs at their gentle reminders. Color darkened her cheeks.

Leaning closer, Sebastian blew a soft, warm breath across her taut nipple. Nothing more, nothing less. Just warm air across her nipple.

A long moan of pleasure left her. Her hand gripped Sebastian's shoulder while her other hand floundered until it found Raphael's wrist and grasped it. Her lashes fluttered closed. Her teeth clamped on her lower lip.

"How I wish to taste you, *gato dulce*," Raphael said.

"Ahh, same here, to see how this bounty of flesh before us tastes, to see her respond to us, that would be such a delight," Sebastian added.

"This..."—she paused, licked her lips—"...this part of my teaching?"

"Oh, I believe we can start this morning with some basics, since you opened yourself up to us in such a delightful way," Raphael said.

"The laws?"

"We will never turn away from you. If we break the laws, it's for passion and our hearts. You will not be left alone in the cold," Sebastian said.

Hillary sucked in her lower lip and nibbled on it. Her breath hitched at the thought. "I...I...I can't. The risk."

The toms exchanged glances.

"Oh, stop doing that, please. You'll give me a complex." She shuddered.

"*¿Qué dijo?*" Raphael asked.

"You exchange glances every time I say something or ask something neither one of you are sure how to answer. It bugs me."

"We're sorry, but that's why we do it. We're not completely sure either. This is all rather new to us."

Her eyebrows lifted.

"Having a female with us. In our lives. In our home."

"In our bed," Sebastian said in a matter-of-fact tone. "It alters everything. We exchange glances and words to make sure we are in agreement to tell you the right thing or give you the correct answer."

"We don't mean to make you uncomfortable," Raphael said.

"I see." She ran a hand over her hair.

"As for the, umm, teaching you and the laws..." Raphael said.

"Yes?"

"Do you trust in us to lead you in the right direction to pleasure all of us and be true to all of us, Hillary?"

Her eyes blinked at Raphael's simple question. Her gaze stayed upon Raphael's face for an elongated time before moving to Sebastian's for an equal moment. Her hands moved and each hand graced one of their cheeks. In turn, she brushed a thumb across their lower lips.

"Lead away, my loves," she whispered. "I place my body in your hands."

"Ah, Hillary, how your words fill our hearts," Raphael said, diving in to capture her lips for a long, passionate kiss.

Her fingers clasped his nape to hold him against her while she extended their kiss. She then turned and met Sebastian's mouth for his kiss, moving her hand to sink her fingers in his soft hair.

She moaned into Sebastian's mouth when she felt Raphael's mouth and hands on her breasts. Sebastian released her mouth as Raphael took her breast fully within his hand. He engulfed her breast in the warmth and heat of his mouth, his tongue curled and laved the nipple before his teeth brushed it. She cried out and arched against them.

While Raphael's hands went to her back and lifted her from the bed, she felt Sebastian tug the robe from her shoulders. As a pair, they removed the robe from under her hips. She barely heard it drop to the floor when Sebastian tossed it aside. Now she felt Sebastian slide closer, feeling how they wore simple boxers as the only barrier between their bodies, so she could feel their heavy erections.

Sebastian's warm hands drew up her sides as Raphael's lips meandered down her body. She mewled and purred under their attention, squirmed and lifted as they found places to excite and arouse her in ways she never knew about.

"Such a noisy little she-cat," Sebastian teased in her ear before nibbling on her lobe. He licked the shell of her ear.

"One wouldn't expect considering how quiet she is during the meetings," Raphael said, his chin nuzzling her belly, above her triangle of curls. He lifted to the side and let his fingers sift through the tiny curls. "Question, Bastian."

"Hmm?"

"Curls or skin?"

"Another issue we never needed to ponder before."

"*Exactamente*, such a delightful issue, too."

"What are we discussing?" Hillary asked.

"Whether we should shave your delightful pussy or leave it alone. I wonder what it would be like to only feel smooth, silky skin when we lick and lap your cream and juices," Raphael said, while his fingers tugged on her curls, eliciting a moan from her.

Groaning at the thought, Hillary closed her eyes and burrowed her head against Sebastian's shoulder. She heard them chuckle at her response.

"Let us enjoy her natural state today, think about it, and decide tomorrow," Sebastian said.

"Excellent idea. It is hair, easy to grow back."

"Hey there, this is my hair we're talking about. Don't I have a say in all of this?" Hillary asked, lifting her head to glance down her body and at the toms.

"No," the toms said in unison.

Hillary groaned and thumped her head back against Sebastian's shoulder. "You two are being impossible."

"Perhaps, but we are enjoying ourselves learning all about you. What excites you? What brings more nectar to moisten your folds?"

Raphael played with the tight curls again as her abdominal muscles tightened and quivered under the creamy skin. His forefinger slipped between the curls and folds and found her heat, wetness, and softness.

"What brings those delightful little noises to your lips," Sebastian teased.

"It absolutely fascinates us to watch."

She arched and gasped at the unexpected touch.

His finger wiggled back and forth against the hood covering her clit.

"Ooooh!" Her eyes closed in pleasure.

"I think she likes," Sebastian said, cupping her breasts again. His thumbs flicked her nipples.

She moaned at the double touch on her body.

Taking it further, Raphael let his finger slip down and swirl in the cream waiting for him. He smiled in a knowing way.

"What is it?" Sebastian asked.

"She's wet for us."

"How much?"

"Deliciously so, her body weeps for us. Here, my Bastian, you can have the first taste of our new mate," Raphael said, pulling his hand from her body and lifting his finger to his partner's lips.

Sebastian raised his eyebrow and smiled.

Hillary opened her eyes and blinked when she heard them talk. Lifting her hand, she wrapped her fingers around Raphael's wrist to steady his hand. "Taste me, Bastian."

"Ah, Hillary, so tempting and delectable." Sebastian kissed her, pulling on her mouth, sweeping his tongue deep inside. When he left her breathing heavily, he turned and brought Raphael's finger, covered with Hillary's cream, into his mouth.

Raphael moaned at the wholesome richness of their gorgeous feline. The very essence of their delectable beauty. His tongue rasped against Raphael's finger, then curled around the tip to make sure he got every drop.

"Well?" Raphael questioned.

"Like nothing we've tasted before, my partner. She's delightful. Perfect in every way. You must try for yourself," Sebastian said, licking his lips as he pulled back.

Hillary chuckled at their reaction to her. "Am I addictive?"

"Oh yes, like catnip," Sebastian said, hugging her tight. He pressed a series of kisses to her neck and jaw.

Leaning her head to the side, she laughed, bringing a hand up to cup his head.

"May I taste you, *querida*?" Raphael asked, shifting between her legs. He carefully opened her legs wider to accommodate his legs, stopping her laughter and play with Sebastian.

She turned her head to stare down at him. "What are you doing?"

"He's going to taste you in the most pleasurable of fashions. You will love us doing this to you. More than anything else in the world," Sebastian whispered.

"He's opening my legs. He is going to look at me…"

"We both will. We're your lovers."

She whimpered. Her body tensed under their gaze and hands.

"Oh, Hillary *dulce*, no, no," Raphael said.

"Ssh, ssh. There is no need to tense up. Not with us. We're not going to hurt you. Only pleasure," Sebastian said. He nuzzled her cheek, her hair.

She nibbled on her lower lip.

"Close your eyes, Hillary, listen to my voice. I will not let anything bad happen, nor will Raphael. Now, turn back around."

She shifted a frantic gaze to Sebastian, and then did as he asked.

"Close your eyes. Take a deep, relaxing breath and let it out slowly."

Again, she did as Sebastian said, in his low, calm tone.

"Good, that's our beautiful kitty. Take another breath. Listen to my voice. Feel my body against yours. Feel my touch." His fingers moved against her breasts, belly, and thighs until soft moans replaced the frantic whimpers. "That's our lovely kitty. Keep breathing. So, beautiful, how does this make you feel?"

She moaned, whimpered now in need for more rather than in fear.

"Good. Now, I want you to relax your hips and legs, darling. Open up for him." His hands moved down her body to her inner thighs. He applied slight pressure to guide her.

With a relaxing sigh, Hillary opened her hips for her lovers and let Raphael spread her legs. She felt his warm skin brush against hers while he settled between her thighs. His broad hands curled around them, then her butt. She whimpered at the sensations wringing through her at the differences between their skin textures, the gentleness, and the sensitivity and pleasure of the nerves he fired off with the slightest touch. Her hips arched off the bed when he touched the moist folds.

She cried out, her eyes opening and finding Sebastian's.

"This is where he was before, when he gave me your taste. Now let him in further, something you've never experienced before, sweet kitty," Sebastian said, capturing her lips for a long kiss.

She screamed in pleasure into Sebastian's mouth when Raphael's fingers opened her moist folds and the flat of his tongue found her taut clit poking out from its hood. Her legs became restless under the sensations and she wrapped them around his body to hold on to him. She broke from Sebastian's kiss.

"Oh sweet Goddess," she said in between heavy breaths. She lifted her head and stared down at the dark head between her legs. She cried out when he continued.

Her head thrashed against Sebastian's chest. He captured her hands and held them in one easy grip while his other arm wrapped around her waist. He anchored her to the bed and the delectable torture of Raphael's mouth.

Chapter 18

It felt like they were all over her. They surrounded her with hands, tongues, and desire in their introduction to their style of lovemaking. Only after they made her orgasm so many times she lost count, her body limp in their arms, Hillary dragged open her eyes when she felt them nestle against either side.

"How can there be possibly more?"

Both toms laughed while they squeezed her in a hug.

"We've barely begun to show you everything, *gato dulce*." Raphael nipped her lips before laving the hurt and soothing with a kiss.

"No more for this morning. Enough play. Time for work," Sebastian announced and slapped Hillary on the butt.

She hissed, giving him a display of sharp fangs.

"Well, now, look who has a temper." He tapped her on the nose with a finger.

Hissing again, she wiggled and shoved out from between them. Free from the jumble of arms and legs, she tossed hair over shoulder, got to her feet, and went to the bathroom. She snatched a bathrobe and the bag of toiletries on the way.

"I expect coffee and breakfast when I get out," she ordered.

She heard laughter when she closed the door.

* * * *

"We created a monster," Sebastian said, lounging on the bed, a satisfied smile upon his face. He trailed his fingers across his partner's arm.

"Hmm, we did indeed. A delightful one." Raphael grinned and plopped a kiss on Sebastian's smiling face.

"We chose well with her."

"Of course, our hearts and cats chose her. They're never wrong."

"Now we need to make it to the full moon."

"Not an issue. All will be well. We'll stay close to home. Keep her safe, us safe, and start to intersect our lives."

Sebastian nodded and stretched his long limbs with a lazy yawn.

Raphael gave his partner a slap on his flat abs and rose off the bed. "Since you caused the hiss, you get breakfast duty."

The other cat snarled. "Hey!"

"Only fair."

Grumbling, Sebastian rolled off the bed, easily landing on his feet with feline reflexes, only to have a powerful arm wrapped around his middle and yank him back to the bed. He snarled when Raphael tucked him under his body.

"Ha, gotcha!" Raphael wiggled his eyebrows.

"What do you think you're doing? We're all starving cats, caffeine deprived, and agitated with sex. You're usually the calm and controlled one of our duo."

"Feeling a little frisky this morning after enjoying our lovely lady." Raphael looked up when the bathroom door opened.

"Oh!" Hillary walked out, damp from the shower, a towel wrapped around her body, ends tucked between her breasts. Another towel in her hands while she tried to dry the wet ends. Her blue eyes widened at the sight of the near-naked males on the bed.

"*Buenos días, querida,*" Raphael said, dropping deliberately on his lover, nibbling along the jaw.

Sebastian groaned, wrapped his arms around Raphael, trailing one hand down Raphael's spine. He grasped the tight butt and squeezed it in play. "He's feeling a little frisky."

"Is that what he calls it?" She strolled over and settled on the edge of the bed.

Raphael chuckled and rolled off his partner. "Just playing." He whacked Sebastian's butt. "Go get dressed and feed us, *amante*."

"What? Why me?" Sebastian demanded.

"Ahhh...you cook better than me."

"Yeah, that's right, you do have a tendency to burn things. I'm not in the mood to eat burned bacon or other stuff."

"I don't go that far!"

Sebastian lifted an eyebrow.

"Okay, perhaps once in a while, but only when you distract me."

"Yeah, yeah. Damn!" Sebastian glanced at Hillary and raised an eyebrow.

She held up a hand and then shook a finger at him. "You're so not asking me to cook on my first morning here."

"You moron!" Raphael smacked the back of Sebastian's head. "Get your ass out of bed and move it!"

Grumbling further, Sebastian curled and rose out of bed. He rubbed his head and then his butt. Then he strolled to the closet to find his favorite pants. "Fine. Fine. The slave cat will start cooking for the master and mistress. Anything else you require of this lowly slave?"

"Does the rest of the house need cleaning?" Raphael called out.

"Not until we move all of my things in from the townhouse," Hillary said, shifting until she lay back against Raphael's hip, enjoying this teasing play.

Sebastian stuck his head out and stared at the lazy couple on the bed. "Already in the works. A couple of toms are on their way to help with that project."

Hillary clapped her hands in an excited fashion. "Excellent."

"What about the bar?" Raphael queried. "Since you seem so full of ideas this *mañana.*"

"Call up Louis and Rosie. Have them take over for the week until the moon is over."

"Sounds like a good plan. I'll talk to the guardians and see what happened after we left. See if someone talked to the alpha about the deal done with her father."

"Yeah, that was on the shady side." Sebastian snorted while he slid jeans over his ass and zipped. He tugged on a T-shirt and pulled his hair in a ponytail after running his hands through the locks while he left the bedroom.

"What was that?" Hillary twisted her head and looked back at Raphael, who grumped and growled after his partner.

"Something about the deal your *padre* made doesn't seem right. We want it looked into to make sure it never happens to another female again and justice is paid for what he and our alpha did to you," Raphael said, leaning over, and kissed her.

Kissing him back, her fingers entwined in his silky hair, Hillary moaned softly. Pulling back, she gave him a small smile.

"Now, rise, get dressed, and let's see what Bastian created for us to eat."

"Sounds like a good idea. Is it true you can't cook?" She rose and went to her suitcase.

"No, I love cooking as much as Bastian. I only adore having Bastian cook for me even more than getting up and doing it myself."

"Oh, you are so mean!" She grabbed a pillow and whacked him over the head.

Laughing, Raphael ducked and rolled away from her playful attack.

"Does he know why you force him out of bed?"

"*Sí*, he adores me." Raphael stretched out on the bed, fawning in triumph over his lover.

Hillary laughed and shook her head. "Don't think you're going to pull a fast one on me, buster."

"Not so soon in our relationship. I'm not that evil."

"Oh?"

"Besides, how can you not help but play with him and tease him. He gets all cute and grumpy when you ruffle his fur. He's *encantador* and irresistible," Raphael said and they laughed together while gathering clothes and dressing for the day.

* * * *

Hours later, thanks to a call for help to other toms, Hillary managed to have all of her personal clothes and items transferred from the townhome to their spacious home. Other than her home office and bookcases, she left the majority of furniture in the townhouse for its next owner. It made the moving a little easier, especially since all the toms brought in extra plastic tubs and boxes for her to pack all her belongings.

After the majority of the move was finished and a huge lunch of dozens of pizzas to satisfy all the feline hunger, the rest of the move belonged to Hillary, Raphael, and Sebastian to sort. Running hands through tousled curls, she went to the living room where the toms had piled everything high. She nibbled on her lower lip while she went to each tub and studied them, tried to figure out what to do.

Raphael leaned a shoulder against a wall, shoved a hand in a pocket. "Did they get everything you wanted?"

"I think we got everything. If not, I'll pick up whatever we missed. Looks like you two will have to make room for one more."

Raphael grinned as he glanced at Sebastian, who entered the room after cleaning up the kitchen from lunch. "Oh, that's not a problem for either one of us. We've been waiting to share our home with you."

"Just like we're waiting to share our hearts and lives with you," Bastian added.

"You two are so sure of yourselves, of this mating, of the trio," she said, dropping to sit on the arm of a nearby chair.

"Are you still worried?" Raphael moved until he stood in front of her, taking her hands in his.

Nodding, she lifted her gaze to meet his.

Sebastian moved from the other side and laid his hands over theirs. "At least until the dance and moon."

"When we're confirmed in front of the clan and have the Goddess bless us, no one can tear us apart," she whispered. "Only the Goddess can protect us from any wrath."

"You won't be afraid to feel something for us," Raphael ventured.

"It's why you hold back in bed," Sebastian added.

Licking her lips, she stared down at their joined hands. "If I give in to our feelings and the moon denies us...I'll be the one turned away. My life will be in ruins."

"We swore we wouldn't turn you away."

"You both are clan, a full part of it. Bastian, you are even from an ancient line. I'm nothing to the clan. Certainly not a part of it, not yet." She pulled her hands from them and moved away. Her arms wrapped around her waist. "I'll have to leave. Clanless. Homeless. A rogue female."

"We'll leave with you."

Pivoting on a foot, Hillary stared at Sebastian who had sworn the unthinkable of a clan guardian.

"*Exactamente*, Sebastian." Raphael nodded twice in a hard, determined fashion. "If the moon denies our relationship after everything we feel and love, we leave together. No matter what, we remain together. Clan or no clan, we remain together."

"But..." Hillary swiveled her head between them.

"Now, are we moving your things to other rooms or leaving everything here?" Sebastian said. "We have three other rooms that we're not really using. Perhaps we can set one up as your home office and another as a personal space for you."

"That's a good place to start. Perhaps the one that lets in the morning light and overlooks the pond. One of the extra rooms and the one next to it, it has the best view." Raphael glanced at her. "What do you think, *querida*?"

She raced to them, throwing her arms around Sebastian's neck, and held on for dear life. Tears came to her eyes when Raphael came up behind her and added his arms around her and Sebastian.

Chapter 19

After her toms banged the corner desk back together and set the bookcases and file cabinets in their various positions, she let them carry in the various office boxes and tubs that contained her paperwork. If Marcus gave her permission, she would love to work from here. She smiled at the thought of how she already considered them her toms. Even without the final dance under the fire moon, they marked her as theirs. They weren't going to give her up. Not under any circumstances would they let her leave their home or hearts.

While the hours passed, she sifted through folders and files, setting them in their rightful places in the cabinets. She hummed and shifted her hips to the music one of the males had set up on the speaker system.

A long arm wrapped around her waist as a tall body stepped behind her. It startled her for a moment before she breathed in Raphael's scent. She let him take the stack of files and set them on the desk. Her hands went up to his neck as he started making them dance in a low, hot rhythm to the beat of the music. His thick cock nestled above the curve of her butt thanks to his height.

"Hmm, Raphael," she whispered as they danced together.

His hands moved down her belly to hold onto her hips, pushing her against his legs as they circled around. Her fingers twined in his dark hair while she tilted her head to the side, letting his lips linger down her throat.

Soon, she felt another pair of fingers trail down her arms, chest, and circle her breasts. Slowly, concentric circles and squeezes by those knowing hands took him closer and closer to her aching, taut nipples. She could feel her clit harden at his touch.

"Well, damn, starting the party without me. That's not fair. Here I was, being a good tom and doing the laundry," Sebastian teased while he worked her breasts.

Lifting heavy lids over passion-filled eyes, Hillary tried to meet his teasing gaze. She felt him step in closer. He fell in step easily with their simple dance motions, his hands teasing her full, engorged breasts and aching nipples.

"Not going to toss another red shirt in the whites again, are you?" Raphael teased in a low tone while his chin nuzzled her shoulder.

Hillary chuckled, keeping one hand in Raphael's hair. She let her other hand drop to caress and hold on to Sebastian's forearm. How she adored touching and holding both of them when they were touching her. She loved the differences between them.

"No, I'm not going to turn your shirts pink again. One little mistake and he still ribs me about it," Sebastian said, shaking his head.

"You both are guardians and alphas. Why are you doing your own laundry? Someone from the clan should be doing it for you," she managed to talk over her arousal. She pulled in a needy breath when Sebastian's hands drifted down her quivering belly to meet Raphael's on her hips.

"At first, when we paired together, no one accepted our request for a housekeeper. Though guardians and toms often paired together, not many declared such relationships like we have before the clan and made them official. It wasn't done," Sebastian said.

"In other words, it pissed off the High Alpha and Council," Raphael said, a low growl accompanying the words.

"No one wanted to get on their bad side, so no one answered our request." Sebastian shrugged. "Over the years, we became self-reliant. Luckily, my mom came to our rescue many a time in the beginning.

She didn't turn away from us, no matter what the High Alpha said. I was her son, and Raphael made me happy."

"It was all she needed to know," Hillary said with a smile.

Sebastian smiled and nodded. "Exactly. She taught us the basics of laundry, housecleaning, decorating, organizing, grocery shopping, and cooking. Over the years, Raphael and I taught ourselves even more in the cooking department."

"We went so far as to going to some of the younger toms, those who are single and living together in groups, and teaching them how to be self-reliant. Showing them the old ways of relying on someone to take care of them is ridiculous and demeaning to that person. If they are old enough to guard the clan, they are old enough to take care of themselves and their home," Raphael added.

"So, what am I to do in this household if you two take care of everything?" Hillary teased.

"For now, nothing. You are our devoted guest," Sebastian said, leaning down to deliver a long, warm kiss to her lips.

Her fingers gripped his forearm as the kiss lingered. Her tongue shyly slipped out, licked along his lips, and met his tongue. When he pulled back, she smiled, blushed, and met his deeper kiss.

"Does that meet with your approval?" Raphael asked after the kiss, nibbling on her ear.

"Oh, I believe I can enjoy that, until I insist upon helping," she said, leaning into his cheek and nibbling when it tickled.

"Excellent. Now, I wish to ask something," Sebastian said, stepping away from them and going to the chair. "I found this amongst your things, darling kitty, and have to inquire about it. I have no idea as to what it is or what it does."

Wrapping his arms around her body in a light hug, Raphael continued the gentle nibbling and licking of her neck and earlobe. Distracted from Sebastian's question, Hillary laughed and wiggled against Raphael's hold.

"Raphael, it tickles. Stop...Raphael..." she tried to say and giggled. "Sebastian, what...I'm sorry, what did you ask?"

Sebastian turned with her body shaper dangling from his fingers.

She stopped cold in Raphael's hold, not responding to his teasing.

"Hillary?" Raphael asked, leaning to the side to look at her.

"Darling, are you all right? What is it about this garment? I have no idea what it is. I found it on the bottom of the suitcase I unpacked for you," Sebastian said. "Raphael, she's pale as a ghost."

"Hillary, *querida?*"

"Where did you find that?" she whispered.

"I told you. The bottom of your suitcase. I unpacked it for you since you were busy in here and I thought I could help. Was that wrong of me?" Sebastian asked.

"That is very personal...You shouldn't..." She reached for the undergarment to snatch it from Sebastian's grip, only to have him pull it away. "Please, give it to me."

"No more secrets between us, Hillary. We all promised that. What is that thing?" Raphael walked them back to the desk until he leaned against it, keeping her between his legs, tugging her with him when she didn't move.

Breaking from his hold, Hillary moved from them and sighed. "It's called a body shaper. It's an undergarment I put on under dresses."

"Body shaper?" the males asked together.

"They help suck in my gut and hips. All the little extra rolls and blobs and stuff I don't like."

"*¿Qué dijo?* Hold on a minute," Raphael said, holding up a hand. He looked from her to Sebastian and back. He shook his head hard and then gazed at her once more. "Suck in your stuff?"

"What is the problem?" She looked at them. "It's a female undergarment, perfectly normal."

"Normal? What is normal about it?" Sebastian demanded.

"You're sucking in your hips and bewitching ass under what? A layer of nylon, spandex, Lycra, and other crap? Because you don't like it? Or you think we don't like it?" Raphael clutched her arm to stop her from drifting away from them.

"We love your natural curves and look, Hillary. Why would you even think to hide them under this? After everything we showed you, loved about you, pleasured, you would hide yourself behind this thing. Why on earth would you do this?"

"You are a luscious pearl."

"Pearl? No. Just full of fat and cellulite," Hillary said, with a sigh. "It jiggles and wiggles like your favorite Jell-O snack. You saw me spread across the bed. It was horrible. My father is forever nagging me to lose the weight."

Raphael pressed his fingers to her lips and shushed her. "He's not here and can't hurt or order you about any longer, *querida.* You may live any way you wish, including how you want your body to look."

She pulled her eyebrows together in a silent question.

"If you like your body this way," he said, "with these delectable curves in all the right places that define you as a woman, please keep them, darling, but no matter what you decide, we will enjoy you no matter what you look like."

She blinked those baby blues, emotions hidden from him, as she leaned back from his fingers. "How could you say what you like and don't like about me?"

"You are our mate. No matter what, we will love you. All of you. That is the way of mates, true mates."

Sebastian nodded as Raphael spoke and then sighed. He stepped over to her other side, curling a hand around her neck. "We truly must do something about your self-esteem, beloved. I believe it is the first thing we'll work on with you."

"Though after we burn that horrible garment. You are never to buy another one of these things again. Ever!" Raphael ordered.

Licking her lips in nervousness, Hillary shifted her gaze back and forth. "What if the dresses don't look as pretty?"

"They're on you, Hillary. That's all we care about when we pick a dress. You."

"Don't ever be afraid, not of us. We'll never hurt you, make fun of you, or say anything harsh about your looks." Sebastian leaned down and kissed her. "Promise us you'll never be afraid of talking to us about your feelings or thoughts. We love you as you are. No matter what."

"No matter what you look like, how you feel, whatever crazy, hormonal mood you're in, we love you and want to be by your side, taking care of you. We're your mates," Raphael added, stepping in for his kiss.

Tears filled her eyes as she buried her face against Raphael's chest, clinging to him and Sebastian, who wrapped his long arms around both of them.

Chapter 20

After some lingering cuddling time, Hillary noticed Raphael stayed in the office, brushing against her, leaving soft kisses and words of encouragement, or helping her out with the various tasks she needed to do to finish the room. For a powerful alpha cat, she wondered how he kept his need for activity calmed enough to be confined.

When the office became finished in another hour or so, Hillary stepped back, arms wrapped around her waist, as she studied everything. She felt Raphael move behind her, enclosing her within his warm hold once more.

"What do you think? Everything feel done in here to your satisfaction, *querida*?" he asked in a rumbled purr.

"Yes, it's a wonderful office. Hopefully, Marcus will approve my working from home after the moon dance. Then it'll be even better." Turning her head against his chest, she lifted her face high enough to kiss his whiskered jaw. "Thank you for helping me and staying close, Raphael. I know you probably had other things to do today instead of spending the entire time with me."

Raphael grumbled at the kiss and then placed a light kiss on her nose. "I enjoyed assisting you. There was nothing else as important as working side by side with you. Nor would I wish to spend it anywhere else."

"Even as an alpha? I know it's hard to keep it contained unless you're doing something more active than working in a confined space."

The elegant Latino shrugged and placed a kiss on her cheek. "I am used to quiet times and confined spaces with the bar, as is my inner feline. Do not worry so about me."

"If you're sure…"

"I am. Sebastian is the same."

"Speaking of him… Where is Sebastian? I haven't heard him moving about."

"He went on an errand and should be back anytime. I chose to stay behind with you while he went shopping."

"Shopping?" She twisted in his arms. "Not for another dress, I hope."

A quick grin flash before it disappeared as he walked out of the room.

"Raphael! What are you two planning?" Hillary quickened her pace to keep up with the smiling alpha tom. "You sneaky tom, get back here!"

* * * *

Neither tom said a word about their mysterious plans for the evening. Nothing while they dressed her in the decadent silk lingerie, then the flirtatious sapphire jersey and silk dress, and clipped the sapphire earrings to her ears. The skirt whirled and flared around her knees when they spun her around. With a grin, Raphael dropped to his knees in front of her and helped her into the matching high heels while Sebastian moved her required pieces of information to the little purse.

They both insisted on her leaving her hair loose and curly around her shoulders. They wanted it flowing, letting their fingers tangle in the dark locks fragrant with her scent. She pushed them out of the way when she stepped in the bathroom to apply makeup.

When she stepped out of the bathroom, she found both of her toms dressed in dark trousers, polished black shoes, and buttoned-up shirts.

Raphael wore a collared cream shirt that only heightened his dark Latino looks with a thin black tie. Sebastian went with a collarless shirt in a mint color to bring out his green eyes, the top buttons left loose. They both pulled on dark dress jackets over the shirts.

"Gorgeous, sweet Hillary," Sebastian said, stepping over, taking her hand and kissing the palm.

"Breathtaking, *querida*," Raphael added, moving to her other side. He took her other hand, kissed her fingers, and rubbed his cheek against them. A gentle purr of respect and adoration rumbled inside his chest as he stayed next to her.

"Where are we going?" She tried to nudge them into telling her what they planned for this evening. They were being so mischievous and playful since Sebastian's return from the store.

"Not saying," Sebastian said.

"Nope. Not a word." Raphael shook his head while tucking her hand around his arm as they led her out of the house.

They continued to play the silent treatment to her questions during the drive. It wasn't back to the restaurant or anywhere within the clan's lands.

"Close your eyes, Hillary, keep it a surprise," Raphael said, sitting next to her in the backseat while Sebastian drove.

"What?" She turned to look at him, watched him raise a satin blindfold and hold it in front of her. "Oh, come on, you two. A blindfold? Really? Is this truly necessary?"

"*Por favor?*"

"Please?" Sebastian pleaded from the front.

Sighing in agreement, Hillary nodded and closed her eyes. She felt the blindfold settled in place by careful hands. It was strange to be in the dark, especially when Raphael leaned in to kiss her, his fingers stroking skin revealed by the flirtatious dress Sebastian had found for her on his shopping spree.

Lifting her hand from her lap, she moved it to find Raphael's face. Her fingers bumped into the smooth, clean-shaven jaw. She smiled and let her thumb stroke against his lower lip.

"This is different, not being able to see you," she said.

"It can give you a bit of freedom in bed, too. A little bit of daring, of the risqué, of the unknown. We can try it if you desire," Raphael murmured.

"It forces you to concentrate on your other senses and not rely on your eyes. Use your hearing, smell, touch, and later even taste to learn your surroundings, Hillary. When we're in human form, we often forget about our other senses. Unlike our feline forms, which use everything," Sebastian said.

"You stopped the car. I can hear and feel that. Are we at our destination?"

"We are, let us help you out."

She felt the brush of the cool breeze against her skin, flirting with the skirt, making it move and float over her bare legs. With their help, she set the heels down first and felt each tom take a hand just by the shape and feel of their hands. She rose from the car and stood between her males.

"Good evening, gentlemen. Welcome back to Twilight. Your keys, Mr. Sebastian?" a man said in a cultured voice.

"Thank you, William. Is Xavier on the floor tonight?" Sebastian asked.

Hillary listened as the gentle clink of keys exchanged hands. She had never heard of a club called Twilight. Her fingers tightened around both her toms' hands.

"The Master is on the floor and will be pleased to see this delightful beauty."

"Not a toy for him, William. This is our new mate to be confirmed at the fire moon under the Goddess," Sebastian said, a possessive tone coloring his words.

"Truly? He will be even more delighted about your news and the sight of her. Take her on in, gentlemen," William answered with a chuckle.

Hillary tilted her head in question. "What is happening? Sebastian? Raphael?"

"Ssh, darling, come with us," Sebastian said before kissing her lips.

"You're not giving me much choice in the matter, blindfolded and everything," she said while walking between them.

"Hmm, you have a feisty lady on your hands. Very interesting."

"Who are William and Xavier? What is Twilight?" Hillary asked after hearing the door close on Steven's laughter.

There was a heavy, throbbing beat of music playing full of passion and need deep within the building. Yet it wasn't loud enough for mere mortals to be aware of it playing. Her toms led her down a hallway of the secular built club.

"Welcome to Twilight, Hillary," Raphael whispered in her ear as he lifted the blindfold from her eyes.

Chapter 21

It wasn't the type of club she expected her toms to bring her to. Gentle plays and swirls of reds, purples, blues, and blacks mixed throughout the club with hints of cream from the furniture, lights, the wall colorings, flooring, and the subtle decorations. There were chains, crosses, whips, rooms cordoned off by glass for others to watch while other rooms had doors for privacy, and a large actual club area with a dance floor and bar.

Ladies dressed in tight corsets and skirts, fishnets, or others in skintight leather outfits, while some wore other beautiful dresses created from an array of fabrics. The gentlemen dressed in a similar range of styles, from the skimpiest of skintight leather pants to full tuxedos. Some even had collars around their necks or wrists.

While she gazed upon the guests with curiosity, others looked upon her and her toms with interest, desire, passion and lust.

"Is this a fetish club?" Hillary pressed closer to Sebastian's taller frame. She felt Raphael move against her back.

"Why yes, little innocent kitty. It is a fetish club. I hope it meets with your approval. I enjoy hearing what newcomers think about my beloved creation," another man answered in a midnight-deep voice that skittered down her spine, hitting all the right nerve endings.

Turning away from Sebastian, Hillary spotted the elegant figure of the tall gentleman standing next to Raphael. Dark blond hair swished to broad shoulders covered in a clean-cut, superbly tailored tuxedo jacket over a creamy white shirt opened at the neck. His face marble pale and hewn strong with a sharp blade of a nose and full lips. Deep, impressive eyes of a rumbling thundercloud captured her attention and held it.

"Gentlemen, who is this divine, succulent morsel you brought into my club?" The man held out a slender-fingered hand to Hillary.

"Her name is Hillary," Sebastian said. "Hillary, I would like to introduce you to Xavier, the owner of Twilight."

"Sebastian?" Hillary asked in a soft tone as she looked at the man's hand and then her toms.

Sebastian nodded in an accepting way that it would be okay for her to touch the other male.

"A pleasure to meet you, Xavier," she said in a low tone.

Xavier drew her away from her toms, spinning her, watching the skirt flare around her legs. "Sebastian, Raphael, I am impressed. She is beautiful. Why have I not met her before?"

"She is a recent transfer to the Fire Moon Clan," Sebastian said, stepping forward, but Hillary noticed how Raphael held him back with a hand on his elbow.

"You should have brought her in sooner, Sebastian."

"Due to clan rules, we couldn't."

"Darn your archaic rules for keeping such beauty away from you and me." Xavier smiled at Hillary. "They do nothing to allow your beloved, gorgeous ones freedom to explore their sensuality at my club. Would you like to explore yourself?"

Entranced by the handsome man in front of her, Hillary barely heard her toms' possessive growl and hiss. She blushed when he drew his fingers down her cheek. "I'm learning to do that with them."

"Really now?" Xavier looked at the toms. "Do you two know what to do with such a beautiful woman in your bed?"

Raphael snarled.

"Down, jaguar. No claws in my club."

"No tricks with her," Raphael warned.

"Are you ordering me?"

"*Sí*," Raphael said with another snarl.

"Definitely impressive. This is a change for the two of you. What am I missing about this new lady of yours?"

The cats snarled.

"Lovely, full curves in all the right places. What a wonderful body, you are a true lady, my dear kitty. Spin again, let me see everything, all these delicious assets you offer," he said, lifting their joined hands and sending her in another simple, slow spin.

When he released her other hand, she felt a warm hand grasp her forearm and tug her away from the elegant stranger. Two sets of arms embraced tightly around her, and she leaned in against twin bodies of powerful strength. Purrs and rumbles vibrated against her skin as smooth jaws rubbed against her. Reassuring scents filled her nostrils, bringing her back to Sebastian and Raphael's arms, back to their love, away from the mesmerizing stranger.

"She is new and innocent to the club. Be cautious with her," Raphael snarled.

"Oh?" Xavier raised a simple eyebrow while arms crossed over his chest.

"We requested courtship before the fire moon, and Hillary accepted. We will become true mates once accepted and bonded by the fire moon dance," Sebastian explained. "She is ours. Not a toy or pet. She is our third mate. Chosen by our hearts, not by the dance."

"Well now, this is a surprise. Come with me, my cats," Xavier said, turning and leading them through the club.

"We wanted to dance," Raphael said.

Coming out of the strange trance, Hillary stopped walking and pulled everyone to a stop around her. She didn't care where they were located inside the club. She tugged her arms from her toms and planted hands on her hips.

Raphael moved toward her to take her in his arms. "*Querida?*"

"Don't you 'darling' or '*querida*' me, Raphael," she snapped, stepping away from his reach.

"Now, Hillary, don't be like this," Sebastian tried.

She sliced a hand through the air to stop Sebastian's placating. "What is going on around here? You, what did you do to me back there?" She lifted a hand and shoved a finger into Xavier's chest.

"Definitely a feisty, wonderful lady, my cats."

Hillary crossed arms under breasts, tapped her foot hard. "Hello, I'm still standing here. I have a mind and will of my own."

Turning to face her, Xavier gave her a true gentleman's bow of respect. "It was a simple calling of power over your jaguar, sweet Hillary. Something I have among all the jaguars of the clan."

Hillary looked at her toms who nodded in agreement. "Did you bring me here to prove something?"

"Only how Xavier can prove to you how beautiful you truly are. If you don't want to believe in our eyes and hearts, listen to Xavier. We've known him for a lifetime and he's never wrong," Raphael said.

"Thank you, Raphael." Xavier smiled and reached out to take Hillary's hands. "Please, my lady, I never meant harm or to take you from your mates. Only to indulge my pleasure of enjoying the beauty of a gorgeous lady." He lifted her hands and kissed her fingers.

Blushing, Hillary tucked her chin in as her lashes drifted down, covering her gaze. "Thank you, Xavier."

"Would you like to continue our evening out with Xavier or return home?" Raphael asked, sliding closer to Hillary, drifting a hand over her back, skin bared to his touch by the low cut dress.

Shifting her gaze to the side, her lashes lifted to reveal her beautiful blue eyes. She leaned into Raphael's fingers when he raised them to caress her cheek. A soft purr rose in her throat.

"Hmm, so pretty," Xavier said.

A blush colored her cheeks.

"It would be rude of us to leave Xavier's hospitality," she said, glancing back at the other man.

"Pshaw! We leave him behind all the time," Sebastian said, nudging Xavier.

"Is that what the two of you call it? Appearing and disappearing whenever you wish?" Xavier asked, crossing arms over his chest after once more releasing Hillary's hands to her mates with ease and care. He nudged Sebastian back with his elbow. "Be grateful I enjoy and care for you two so much to put up with your shenanigans. Not everyone would get away with all that I let you pull off around my club."

"Without us around, it would be rather boring," Sebastian said.

Raphael rolled his eyes, one arm sliding around Hillary's shoulders to pull her in close while Sebastian and Xavier continued to tease and ridicule one another. "What do you say, Hillary? Do you wish to leave?"

Hillary looked at Xavier and Sebastian ribbing and joshing with each other. She enjoyed their antics, but saw both turned with attention on her.

"You know, my dear cat, though I believe your intentions were to show her a delightful evening out and prove how beautiful she is to others, especially me," Xavier said, stepping over to Hillary and Raphael. He gently took Hillary's hands in one of his larger hands while his other hand cupped her chin.

Hillary heard Sebastian's light, possessive growl at Xavier's touch, but saw Raphael shake his head to ask him to hold it back.

"I believe your intentions were met and exceeded this night, correct, my pretty one?"

Under Xavier's attention, she blushed. "Yes. My toms had only the best intentions tonight, not that they went about it in the correct fashion."

"Ah now, Hillary, really…" Sebastian tried and stopped when Hillary glared. He zipped his mouth shut.

When her gaze slid to Raphael, he rocked back on his heels and wisely kept his trap closed.

"Only been with them a couple of days, correct?" Xavier asked.

"Yes, why?" Hillary asked, turning back to Xavier.

"Nothing. Nothing. I must commend you on your excellent control over them," he said with a snicker behind a hand.

Sebastian lifted a lip and snarled at Xavier.

Hillary hissed and whacked a hand against Sebastian's arm to stop him.

Xavier laughed at their exchange. "Raphael, take your mates home. Both of you are to pleasure your most beautiful and beloved lady. That is an order, dearest cat."

"Why tell me?" Raphael asked, eyebrows lifting in surprise.

"You seem the calmest and most levelheaded out of the trio."

"Oh no, that changes in a heartbeat. You know us felines." Raphael grinned and winked.

Shaking his head, Xavier leaned in and pressed a light kiss to Hillary's temple. "It's my dearest pleasure to meet you, sweet Hillary."

"Same with you, Xavier." Hillary blushed and leaned against Xavier.

"You are welcome to Twilight, with or without your mates, at any time. If you need anything, anything at all, please don't hesitate to contact me. Like your mates, I will be at your side in a heartbeat."

"Thank you for that, Xavier, I will keep it all in mind. Especially if these two get on the last edges of my nerves and I need a break from them," she said.

Xavier laughed long once more, ending with another kiss on her temple. "Raphael and Sebastian, hurry, take her home and enjoy her before I steal her from you. Hillary, I find myself unable to resist your charms, but I enjoy my flesh unharmed by claws and my manhood intact, so I bid you a good evening and a pleasant one." With a bow and flourish, he walked away, disappearing into the crowds of the nearby dance floor.

Hillary looked over at her toms and lifted a brow. "Well? You heard him. Take me home and enjoy me."

Her toms burst into chuckles, bowing with their own types of flourishes, wrapped arms around her waist, and led her away.

Chapter 22

Body trembling, sweaty limbs tangled with others and the sheets, Hillary nuzzled her cheek on Sebastian's shoulder. The clever sensual things these toms could do with her body she couldn't even imagine before they came into her life. Lifting her head, she pressed her lips to his warm, silken flesh.

Then she arched her back when Raphael stroked his fingers down her lower spine, causing her to moan and purr all at the same time. Turning to look over her shoulder, she gave him a lazy smile and accepted his kiss.

"*Querida*," he whispered in his Spanish flair she adored.

Lifting a hand, she tangled her fingers in his dark hair and tugged him down for another lingering kiss, tongues dancing, playing. She felt Sebastian's hands move over her body and Raphael's at the same time, not leaving either one of them without his touch.

Soon, they settled back down, Hillary against Sebastian, with Raphael against her. She loved being sandwiched between their strong, steady bodies, enclosed in their arms and love. She could feel their hearts beat against their chests and into hers.

"Hmm, this is wonderful. Don't ever want it to change," she said.

"The Fire Moon is tomorrow. We dance then to make our commitment to one another permanent before the clan and our Goddess," Sebastian said.

"It's tomorrow? I can't believe it is here. So soon." Hillary tilted her head to look at him.

"This is what we want to happen," Raphael said, his fingers moving through her hair.

"Oh yes, this is what I want. More than ever, I want to dance with the both of you, for the both of you before the eyes of our Goddess, if not in front of the clan. I don't think our kin are ready to receive us." Hillary returned to her place upon Sebastian's chest.

"Perhaps, perhaps not, but it isn't their choice. Only the Goddess may look deep within our hearts and approve our union," Sebastian assured in his calm manner that got all three of them to chuckle.

The doorbell buzzed a few times to disturb their peace.

"Can we ignore it?" Hillary asked after a little moue of displeasure.

Hard pounding knocks on the door were her answer. They were loud enough to reverberate through the house and into the coziness of the upstairs master suite.

"Guess not. Hell, now what is going on in the world that we can't get a few moments of quiet?" Sebastian grumbled as he rolled from his lovers. He snatched a pair of jeans from a pile on the floor and tugged them on. "I'll check it out."

"Want me to come with you?" Raphael sat up with Hillary curling against him. The sheet and blanket tenting around them.

"No, hopefully it won't be long and you can keep the bed warm." Kissing his fingers and waving them in their direction, Sebastian left the room.

Leaning against Raphael's warm chest, Hillary listened to Sebastian's footsteps on the stairs. She knew Raphael also attuned himself to Sebastian's movements as they heard the door opening and an exchange of voices.

"Raphael, Hillary, could you come down, please?" Sebastian called up the stairs in a louder voice.

After glancing at each other, they left the comfort of the warm bed. Hillary pulled on a simple cotton jersey dress over panties, leaving her hair in disarray from her lovers' fingers. She saw Raphael pulled on dark jeans and nothing else. She took his hand and they went down the stairs together.

In the living room, they saw Sebastian sitting on the arm of the loveseat, which he indicated for them to use. They felt the almost overwhelming power of a potent alpha within the room and turned in near unison to see the kin male sitting in the armchair.

Rising gracefully to his six-four height, shoving a hand through red brown hair that dropped over his face, blue gray eyes sparkling under thick lashes, the alpha nodded his head in respect to them. "Greetings, Raphael, Hillary. Please accept my apologies for disturbing you this afternoon."

Hillary glanced at Sebastian and then Raphael before looking back at the unknown male. Her fingers tightened around Raphael's, not letting go of his hand for anything. She held her ground, though, against the power of this alpha male.

"Hello and I will accept...after we know who you are and why you are in our home?" Raphael said, not accepting anything at face value.

"Raphael..." Sebastian warned.

Hillary tugged Raphael to the loveseat and settled down. She forced Raphael to sit next to her, quelling the argumentative comment she could feel inside him, and reached a hand to Sebastian.

"I don't blame you for being suspicious. I would be if I were in your position. My name is Alexander. Alex among us," the intriguing male said.

"Alex what?" Raphael said.

"Raphael!" Hillary nudged him in the side with her elbow. "Manners."

"I have none. I'm your future mate and protector. That comes before grace and manners," Raphael said.

Harrumphing, Hillary looked at Sebastian for help and saw the same expression on his face as Raphael's face. "Oh sweet Goddess, save me from overbearing and testosterone-driven males."

Alex chuckled behind a hand.

"Don't think I'm not including you in the group," she said, narrowing her gaze upon him. "Spill it, male. Who are you? Why are you here?"

"She always like this?" Alex asked the males.

"Since we met her, yup," Sebastian said. "We find ourselves rather enjoying it, too. Keeps us in line."

"She is sitting right here as usual," Hillary said, dropping their hands and folding them under her breasts. Crossing her legs, she tapped a bare toe in the air to show her frustration. Unfolding her arms, she pointed a finger at Alex. "You. Talk."

"Alexander Thurston, miss. Middle son of Irvine Thurston," Alex said, leaning forward, forearms resting on his knees.

"Thurs—what?" Raphael nearly swallowed his tongue. "What the hell?" Surging forward, he started to rise until Sebastian reached behind Hillary and yanked him down. "Bastian?"

Alex held up his hands. "I'm not here to cause trouble, please, no alarm."

"*Sí*, right. Do you know what your father and her *padre* did to her?"

"Raphael... Please, there is no need," Hillary said, trying to calm her Latino male.

"It's why I'm here. Collin Thompson told me everything that happened at Serenade and what happened at Hillary's townhome. After a thorough investigation and then interrogation of both alphas by Collin and myself, I..." Alex dropped his head in a hand. "I'm ashamed of my father's actions and behavior."

"Why docs this bring you here?" Sebastian asked.

"One, to apologize to Hillary on behalf of my family's interference in her life and the pain it caused her," Alex said, lifting his head to look at Hillary. "I truly am sorry for what my father did, Hillary. He should never have considered such a horrendous scheme and conditions your father came up with, let alone gone through with them. No daughter, no child, should ever be placed at the mercy of an overreaching, power-hungry parent."

"Thank you for your apology," Hillary said.

"Second thing is another apology about the horrendous behavior of my youngest brother, Josh, concerning his care of you after your previous dance then his untimely mating to Belinda Alcott. My brother was always the weak one, following my father's every word, along with any crook of Belinda's finger." Shoving a hand through his hair, Alex let out a long sigh. "My family, may the Goddess forgive me, but they are horrid wretches to deal with at most times. I guess it's why I disappeared from the clan for so long, to get a little peace, but I couldn't run away from my duties. Anyway, I will deal with my brother and his mate after the Fire Moon. They will make retribution to you, I promise."

"There really is no need for that. I just want it done and over."

"If that is your wish, I will still handle them my way and perhaps transfer some financial retribution in exchange for a verbal apology to you in front of the clan. Will that be acceptable?"

Hillary glanced at her males. Sebastian nodded and she sighed. "Very well, if I must."

"Good, good, it would make me feel somewhat better about all the harm my family has done." Alex smiled as he rubbed his hands together in a distracted fashion.

"Is there anything else?"

"Ahh, yes. I relieved my father of his status and became High Alpha ad interim. My father and Mr. Kearney are in a secured cell with guardians selected by Collin. They will remain there until a judicial council can be convened to determine a final judgment and sentence."

"I'm sure that isn't making you the popular one in your family," Hillary said.

A small grin curled up one side of Alex's mouth. "No, but then I was never the popular one in the family."

"What about our dance?" Raphael demanded.

"Oh, yes, of course, the Fire Moon Dance for the three of you will go on tomorrow. You three will be the only ones who will dance under the moon and our goddess. I told Collin to spread the word amongst the clan," Alex said. "About this...courtship law you found, Sebastian."

"What about it?" Sebastian looked at the other male.

"Excellent work on discovering the original laws of our Goddess. I never did agree with this sexual dance and constant shifting of partners or forcing of one partner on another. I believe the courtship law should be reenacted immediately and the other dance removed," Alex said.

"Courtship law does include no actual penetrative sex. There can be sexual play up to, but not including, penetration. It's quite different from the dance," Sebastian said, making that rule quite clear to the alpha.

"I'll make sure it's understood," Alex said with a smile as he rose to his feet.

Hillary rose to her feet and stepped to Alex. Feeling free of all her fears after his warm words, she lifted on bare toes and kissed his cheek.

It rather startled him. She could see it in his expression and the way he looked down at her, a questioning expression upon his face.

"Thank you for everything and coming here to speak with us," she said.

"I would have it no other way, Hillary. It was a pleasure and delight to meet you. By the way, I proclaim you a full and honorary member of our clan with all the rights and benefits that go along with the membership."

Her jaw dropped. "I'm what..."

Alex chuckled and kissed her cheek. He took her hands in his and stretched them to the side, gently placing each one in a strong male hand. "I'll let your beloved males explain everything. I look forward to enjoying your dance tomorrow under our Goddess and the Fire Moon."

"Thank you for everything, High Alpha," Sebastian said, holding out a hand, his voice full of reverence for the other male.

"Nothing more than all of you deserved. I'll leave you to enjoy the rest of your evening," Alex said, shaking hands with Sebastian and then Raphael, and headed to the door.

Still dazed at the thought of being a full-fledged member of the clan, Hillary smiled at her males. She saw Alex stop at the door, glance back at them. She caught a glimpse of a wistful look move across his face before he opened the door and left.

"He did say what I think he said?" she said, tilting her head.

Both of her males laughed, hugging her close in a tight sandwich.

Chapter 23

It was the time of the Fire Moon Dance.

This month, the moon rose high and took on a reddish hue. This was a true fire moon. Those who found their mate under this moon would be truly blessed.

Ancient and new drums of various styles, sizes, and shapes gathered in one section of the honored and revered section where the dances took place every moon. The beat turned heavy and sensual to represent the male half of the couple. Well-practiced hands and fingers came down against the stretched, honed leather and skins.

The other gathered males of the clan, now stripped down to boxers or of all clothing, stomped their feet to the ancient rhythm of the drums, passed down through generations and legacies of the clan. Sweat and oil greased their muscles, making each curve prominent against the warm tones of the skin, showing their masculinity to the sensual feminine gazes looking upon them.

Instead of all the available males dancing around the roaring bonfire, all eyes of the clan moved to the two trails leading into the forest. One trail for the male side and one for the female side of the mating union of the Fire Moon Dance under the eyes of the Goddess and the clan. Only this dance would be special and unique. Two powerful male guardians were dancing to join with one female kin.

Out of the forest on the masculine trail, stomping and clawing the ancient trail trod upon by so many before them, appeared two graceful felines. One was as dark as the night from nose to tail with his rosette patterns darker than the rest of the fur. The second was larger than the first with golden brown fur and the black rosettes of the proud jaguars that filled the clan.

They walked side by side down the path to the beat of the drums, as they had for the last few decades of their lives. Together as guardians and lovers toward their future as a triad.

Reaching the end of the trail, they circled each other, brushing from nose to tail, then leaned their heads back, screaming their intentions to the Goddess and their mate. Turning, they looked to the feminine trail.

Now mixed within the powerful beat of the drums came the higher, feminine-pitched sounds of the beautiful flutes. With everything from tin flutes to expensive flutes to join in the celebration to create the dance. Along with the flutes came the elegant sounds of the simple cherished fiddles passed through generations and the finest violins gathered to represent the female.

A slender, pitch-black jaguar danced and trotted in an elegant fashion down the feminine trail. A lei of ivory roses and blue wildflowers draped around her neck. Her long tail waved high in the air as she moved to the music.

When she reached the end of the feminine trail, she danced toward her males. Moving between them, she brushed along them from nose to tail, exchanging scents.

After they passed one another, they transformed into their human forms, naked for all to see and before the eyes of their Goddess. Only the lei of flowers, a gift from her males, remained draped around Hillary's neck.

As the drums picked up, so did Sebastian and Raphael when they twirled, thumped, and ground the steps as they circled around the bonfire. Sweat glistened off hard, muscular bodies as they thumped, thrust, and twisted with the steps, simulating the sensual movements of sex.

Opposite of the hard thrust and grind of the males, Hillary's body moved in a graceful, swirling motion in a series of widening circles around the males. She dipped, waved, and rolled her arms and upper body around herself and them. Lifting one foot up with the twirl, she continued the dance around the bonfire with her males, brushing skin against skin, hands against hands, eyes gazing upon one another.

As their dance circled around to bring them closer to the clan, everyone saw the glow of the bonfire change under the brilliant deep scarlet full moon hanging in the sky. It morphed from its usual colors to the single scarlet color of the Fire Moon, signaling the Goddess was looking down upon the dance.

Slowing their dance, Hillary stepped between her males, took each of their hands. As one, they stepped into the powerful blaze to complete the ritual.

Within the flames, Sebastian step against Hillary's back and Raphael her front. They enclosed her within their arms and all looked up at the sky and the heavy moon. They raised their left hands, clasped their fingers together, and watched the flames wrap around their skin, caressing them with its warm glow, flickering lightly, but never burning them, more like a kiss from their beloved goddess. When the flames retreated, a beautiful henna-colored cuff decorated their wrists.

When they stepped out of the flames, the bonfire returned to normal colors. The music quieted as everyone waited for the couple to present themselves to the High Alpha and the rest of the kin and see if the Goddess had accepted their dance and triad.

Their mating cuffs glowed brilliant against their skin for a few brief moments, pulsing with their heartbeats as acting High Alpha Alex Thurston stepped forward and bowed to the new triad. He turned and raised his hands.

"May I present our newest triad—Sebastian Heywood, Raphael Salazar, and Hillary Kearney. Our Goddess accepted and marked them with their mating cuffs. As acting High Alpha, I welcome them into our clan," Alex announced to the entire clan. "The Fire Moon Dance has come to a close for this equinox."

Moving forward, robes draped over her arms, Valerie kissed their cheeks in congratulations while she handed them each a robe. "Marcus is waiting with the golf cart to take you home for your private ceremony."

"Thank you for being a part of this," Hillary said, kissing Valerie's cheek after Sebastian helped her into the robe.

"It was my pleasure, sweet one. Gentle cats, take good care of her." Valerie placed a hand on each of the males' cheeks and then slipped into the night to mingle with the other kin.

Each male wrapping an arm around Hillary's waist, they walked together to the golf cart and the ride home. Some kin came forward to congratulate them and shake their hands. Others contemplated the beautiful dance.

"How dare you, a nothing newcomer, get a mating mark! You ruined everything," a familiar, whiny female cried out above all the congratulations.

Hillary turned in her males' protective arms and saw a bitter, furious Belinda shoving Josh away before stomping toward Hillary. So stunned by Belinda's reaction to the dance, Hillary didn't see her enemy raising a hand and slapping her. Her head shifted to the side, her cheek stinging from the force of the slap.

Growls and snarls filled the air. Belinda screeched in fury, her hands turning into paws filled with sharp claws as a pair of guardians grabbed her and pulled her away.

"Bitch! You little bitch, you ruined everything! This is supposed to be my moon, my dance, my clan! It was promised to me," Belinda screamed, fighting against the guardians. "How could you get the mark? Damn you, Josh, you promised me the mark and everything! You lying bastard!"

Curled against Sebastian's body, Raphael standing in front of them, Hillary moved her jaw as Sebastian gently touched her cheek. She winced against his fingers, the sting still sharp and flared throughout the side of her face. She lifted her gaze to meet his worried one and then shifted to find Raphael's upset expression.

"*Querida*, are you all right?" Raphael turned to face her and Sebastian.

"I'll be fine. Let me see her," Hillary said, straightening in Sebastian's hold. She raised a hand to Sebastian's cheek. "Release me, love."

Sebastian nodded and opened his arms. "We're not moving any further."

"Nor do I want you to. After I deal with her, we're going home." Hillary kissed his cheek and then Raphael's. She looked at Belinda. "Wait, Collin, don't take her."

"She attacked you. It's cause for immediate seclusion and a trial," Collin said.

"You can hold and wait until Hillary has her say, Collin," Alex said, stepping forward.

"How can you let this happen to my mate? Alex, please, release Belinda now," Josh said, pushing forward. "She only reacted to provocation by this bitch."

"What provocation, Josh? No one saw Hillary do anything. It was Belinda who acted first and in a derogatory manner," Alex said and waved to another pair of guardians to take hold of his brother. "I'm sick and tired of dealing with you and your bitch. Either the two of you apologize to Hillary and her mates for trying to ruin this night or I'll have both of you locked into seclusion. I do mean seclusion, in separate cells, Josh."

"Father will never let this stand."

"Father is going to be busy answering for his own crimes and will not get your ass out of this mess. I wouldn't count on Mother's help either. I've already spoken with her. She values her comforts a little too much to go against my orders and wishes."

Hillary placed a hand on Alex's shoulder. "Enough, Alex, please," she said in a low voice.

Alex turned to look at her, concern in his gaze. "Not this time, Hillary. I will not, can't stand by this time."

Pulling in a deep breath, Hillary exhaled slow and steady. She turned to face Belinda, who continued to screech and fight. "You are a conniving, conceited, self-serving cat who has no care for anyone else but her own self, Belinda. You're a manipulative bitch and everyone in this clan knows about your scams, schemes, and acts of jealousy and hatred against every other female who dares to try and make a match or do something that gives them a step over you. That is why our Goddess will never grant you a mating mark. You will never deserve the mark or anything else from her."

"As if you know anything, little bitch. You would never have the nerve to say that to me if you didn't have those two behind you," Belinda said.

"Oh yes, I would. They taught me to find the strength and confidence within myself. All they gave me was love. Something you'll never know." Hillary shook her head. "I feel sorry for you, Belinda, condemned to be forever selfish and kept locked away from the love of our Goddess. That is the worst punishment any kin could ever receive."

Belinda screeched in pain and distress at finally knowing she had lost her power within the clan. Finally, the guardians managed to yank and pull her away from the crowd, with Josh falling behind them.

"Once again, I apologize to the three of you for their behavior," Alex said.

Reaching out, Hillary curled a hand around Alex's cheek. "There is no reason for you to apologize for them when they are more than capable of commanding their own behaviors and morals. All here have now seen how they have control over neither. I hope the clan can see the truth behind them."

"If not, it will come to them." Alex brought up his hand and gently squeezed hers before releasing it and Hillary back to her mates. "Now, I don't want to keep you from your beloveds. Time for the three of you to go home. Go and enjoy one another. I will clear up the mess and finish the dance."

"Thank you, Alex. One day, I hope you will know the blessings and grace of our Goddess," Hillary said.

"I wish for the same." Alex nodded to her and the powerful guardians she took as her mates.

Sebastian and Raphael bowed back to the new High Alpha, pressing a hand to their chests out of respect for him. They each wrapped an arm around Hillary's waist and led her to the waiting golf cart that would escort them to their house, driven by Marcus.

Chapter 24

Closing the door to their home and locking the world out, Sebastian leaned against the door, crossing arms over his chest, and stared at his mates. Huge smiles spread across all their faces. They fell into each other's embraces. Pure laughter rang into the air. Rushing up the stairs, they tripped over each other, tugging and pulling their robes to let them fall to the floor, then tumbled onto the bed. Lying in a pile of tangled limbs, they placed their arms next to one another to reveal their mating marks.

"How many receive this from the Goddess?" Hillary asked as she studied hers.

"Not too many, even if they do enter the flames. They are accepted by her, but she doesn't mark them as hers," Sebastian said.

"So, why were we marked?"

"The Goddess has her reasons. No one can explain why she does what she does."

Raphael trailed his fingers over her bare hip with a sensual smile. "Are we going to talk about our Goddess all night or enjoy our delicious mate, Sebastian?"

"Hmm, all restraints are removed from our relationship," Sebastian said.

"Then I believe we are all wearing a little too much right now," Hillary said, her husky voice curling around their senses. She sat up between them, placing a hand on each chest, one covered in swarthy skin of Latino heritage while the other was golden in coloring. "I still can't accept one of you inside my ass. It's too much for me."

"Nor will we push you this night. There are other ways we can all join together and Raphael and I are used to loving one another."

"Again, too much talking," Raphael said, impatient to begin loving his mates. "Lie back, Hillary, open those delicious knees and let us taste your cream. We can smell how wet you are." He closed a hand around the base of his swollen cock jutting out from his body, the crown slick with his pre-come. Gripping with a firm stroke, he moved his fingers up over the stiffness and groaned at the sensations. "Come on, *querida*. We need you so much."

Stretching out against the pile of pillows, Hillary let her knees fall open, revealing the moist slit between them. Smiling up at them, she moved her hands through her hair, fluffing it over the pillows before letting them linger down the nape of her neck, teasing her mates.

Both of her toms were on their knees, holding errant, swollen dicks in their fists while they watched with eager looks as her hands cupped her small breasts, thumbs flicking her taut nipples. She squeezed and pushed her breasts together, molding them with care and greed as she writhed in front of them. Then her hands continued to travel down her body. One single finger circled and played with her belly button, another little taunt to them.

Sebastian grunted and shifted hands on his cock. His freed hand now caressed Raphael's slim, solid flank. "We taught this minx far too well how to manipulate and tease us, my love."

Tilting his head against Sebastian's shoulder, Raphael nuzzled him with his lips and purred in appreciation of the delicious sight in front of him and Sebastian's touch upon his body. His lips smiled as a groan left him when Sebastian pushed his hand away from his cock and replaced it with his fingers.

"Which one of us should slide inside her wetness first?" Sebastian asked.

"Hmm, she will be tight and slick with her cream. It will feel like heaven for both of us, no matter who loves her first or second," Raphael said.

Her hands stoked across her lower stomach, teased the curls her males still couldn't decide whether to shave clean or leave alone. Her fingers caressed her thighs, the sensitive line where hip and thigh met, and her back arched as she moaned softly with the raised sensation.

Both her males groaned with the same need, wanting to caress her, but held back, watching her touch herself.

"Ahh, *querida*, how you glisten. How you smell with your desire and need," Raphael growled.

Hillary spread the thickened vulva lips for them, shoved two fingers inside her and moaned at the slight stretching. She pulled more cream out and spread it over her taut pearl and reddened lips.

"How you tease us with your cream," Raphael said.

Leaning closer, Sebastian closed his eyes as he pulled her sensual scent into his nose and licked his lips. He felt Raphael's fingers drift through his hair and opened his eyes to turn his gaze to their Latino lover.

"Lick her cream, *mi amante*, taste her sweet juices," Raphael said.

"How can I not comply with that order?" Sebastian teased with a smile and lowered his head to her. Cupping his hands under her butt to lift her, he licked once up her wet slit, making her cry out in need. Then he sucked on her clit.

Crawling on the bed, Raphael stopped to suckle her breast in his mouth. His other hand cupped and massaged the other tender globe. He held her in place by moving his hand to her belly when she lifted her hips and thrust against Sebastian's mouth. Rising to his knees, he held his cock next to her mouth. He caressed a finger down her cheek.

She turned her head and opened her mouth, relaxing her jaw. She lifted her gaze to meet his. When he cupped his cock, the purpled head brushed against her lips. Sassy with need, she poked her tongue out to lick him, tasting the salty pre-come leaking from the slit.

"Ahh, damn it," he said, jerking away at the fierce jolt of sensation.

Licking her lips, she moaned when Sebastian shoved two fingers deep inside and found the sweet G-spot. She cried out when he began a series of pats and rubs and strokes against the sensitive area and mixed it in with sucking her clit.

Then Raphael thrust forward, his cock sliding in and out of her mouth. The salty taste of his pre-cum lined her tongue, giving her just a taste of him. She whimpered around his thick cock, enjoying the feel of him in her mouth as she equally embraced what Sebastian did to her pussy. His long, slow strokes into her mouth kept her lips stretched thin so she couldn't suck him hard, and each deep end had him almost hitting her throat. She kept her jaw relaxed as they taught her, but she hummed with pleasure and set off a small vibration around his cock that caused him to shudder and swear.

Sweat rolled off his forehead as Raphael tried to keep his strokes steady, giving them all pleasure, to make it last. "Want more, *querida?*"

Mouth full of his cock, she couldn't reply, but lifted her gaze to meet his. His hand fisted in her dark hair, holding the back of her head to support it and hold her steady for his cock. She whimpered and moaned.

"Join us, *mi amante*, make us one," Raphael said.

Hillary felt the bed shift by her hips and Sebastian pulled his fingers from her pussy. She whimpered at the emptiness in her channel.

"I have you, darling," Sebastian said, his deep voice soothing, as his hands moved over her thighs.

She then felt the smooth flared head of his cock pressed firm against her opening. She moaned as Sebastian rocked back and forth, his cock moving inch by inch into her wet channel, opening her sensitive tissues to his length and girth. He let her get used to the feeling of his presence, his thumb flicking her clit, before he thrust forward in a single motion. Then she found herself stuffed to the hilt with his penetration.

Moaning around Raphael's cock, her lips relaxed to suck and hold on to him, Hillary concentrated on the feeling of both her mates' penetrations into her body for the first time. Tiny vaginal muscles squeezed, relaxed, and pulsed around Sebastian's cock, feeling one for the first time.

"Oh damn, so tight, so good," Sebastian said, leaning forward and kissing Hillary's collarbone. "So warm and wet, like a silken glove. It's beautiful."

"Can't wait, *amante*, I'm so there. So is Hillary, I can feel her..." Raphael said, his voice thick with his exertions. He felt Hillary move a hand to grip his ass. Her nails dug into his skin as he continued to piston into her mouth. He growled when her tongue flicked against the base of the flared crown when it passed with every thrust.

Gripping hold of her hips, Sebastian lifted them and began to match Raphael's every stroke with his in her channel. He pumped himself harder between her legs, his pelvis hitting her taut clit, rubbing it with every stroke.

Hillary couldn't get enough of them. Her feline yowled for her mates. With one hand on Raphael's ass, she moved her other hand to Sebastian's shoulder and dug in with her nails. Needing that final connection, she felt the sensations rolling through her body. Her pulse hammered ferociously under her skin. Sweat beaded across her body, dampening her hair.

Finally, the near-vicious climax rolled through her. She grunted and screamed around Raphael's cock. Her channel convulsed and gripped Sebastian's cock, triggering his own release deep inside her. Above her, Raphael joined in with his own scream of release, and she greedily swallowed his spurts of semen and cleaned him.

When they both pulled away from her, Raphael slid down and Sebastian slid up with her sandwiched between them. Hillary purred in contentment. She caressed their cheeks, kissing each in turn, watched them kiss one another.

"I love you, my beautiful mates, thank you for choosing me," she said.

"The Goddess chose you for us. We only followed her blessings," Raphael said.

"And the Fire Moon," Sebastian said.

"Hmm, an excellent dance."

"An exceptional dance."

The three kin mates snuggled in contentment, their mating marks united for the Goddess to shine down on them in the moonlight.

THE END

NICOLEDENNIS.CO.CC

ABOUT THE AUTHOR

Ever the quiet one growing up, Nicole Dennis often slid away from reality and curled up with a book to slip into the worlds of her favorite authors. Since then, she's had a fascination with fantasy, paranormal and the never-ending appeal and beauty of romance. It seems only natural all of these loves would come together in her writing from simple stories for her dolls until the summer when her aunt introduced her to Silhouette Presents novels. What a world that opened.

It's been non-stop since that hot New Jersey summer. It's only gotten worse (in a good way). Now she's created a personal library full of novels filled with dragons, fairies, vampires, shapeshifters of all kinds, and romance. Always she returned to romance. Still, there were these characters in her head, worlds wanting to be built on paper, and stories wanting to be told and she began writing them down whether during or after class. She continues to this day. Only recently has it begun to become fruitful, spreading out to let others read and enter her worlds, meet her characters, and see what she sees. No matter what she writes, her stories of romance with their twists of paranormal, fantasy, and erotica will always have their Happily Ever Afters.

She currently works in a quiet office in Central Florida, where she also makes her home, and enjoys the down time to slip into her characters and worlds to escape reality from time to time. At home, she becomes human slave to two crazy cats—an angelic red tabby and a semi-demonic black-orange calico.

She loves to hear from readers and fans, so don't be shy. Find her on the 'net or send an email at nicoledennis.author@gmail.com. Find her at the following links:

Facebook:
http://www.facebook.com/#/profile.php?v=info&ref=profile&id=137
1949975
Facebook Page:
http://www.facebook.com/#!/pages/Nicole-Dennis/107177776016259
Goodreads:
http://www.goodreads.com/group/show/50397.Q_A_with_Nicole_De
nnis

Also by Nicole Dennis

Siren Allure: *Unholy Angel*

Available at
BOOKSTRAND.COM

Siren Publishing, Inc.
www.SirenPublishing.com

CPSIA information can be obtained at www.ICGtesting.com
Printed in the USA
LVOW090433271011

252304LV00004B/22/P